RED LINE VIOLATION

KADE VANCE - The Runway Rogue
Book EIGHT

A Flying Adventure Novel

By Kevin Seney

Lucas Publishing - Lucas Media Company

Kalispell, Montana

Copyright © 2026 by Kevin Seney

All rights reserved. No part of this publication may be reproduced, distributed, or transmitted in any form or by any means, including photocopying, recording, or other electronic or mechanical methods, without the prior written permission of the publisher, except in the case of brief quotations embodied in critical reviews and certain other noncommercial uses permitted by copyright law.

Printed in the United States of America.

ISBN: 9798242457089

Lucas Publishing - Lucas Media Company

Kalispell, Montana

since 1899

www.LucasMediaCompany.com

Acknowledgments

To my family—my home base, my compass, and the reason every journey matters.

*To my wife, **Carrie**—my brave beauty—your strength, grace, and quiet fire steady me more than any instrument ever could. Your voice lives in these pages, especially through my female voices, who carry your truth, courage, and heart.*

*To **Alicia and Jessica**, my first copilots—thank you for learning to fly beside me. Watching you chart your own courses has been my greatest pride.*

*To **Emma, Katie, Gwynn, and Rachel**—your curiosity, humor, and kindness fuel everything I create. You remind me daily that imagination is a responsibility —and love is a practice.*

*To **Maggie and Aspen**, our loyal German Shorthaired Pointers—thank you for reminding us to chase the wind, trust our instincts, and never ignore a good trail.*

This book was written across a season of movement and return—summer in the mountains, autumn in Europe, and winter settling quietly back home in Utah. It carries pieces of all of you, moments we'll always remember, and stories we're only beginning to tell.

With all my love,

Dad

Dedicated to The Seney Twins:

Frank & Fred

Pilots, Pharmacists, Community Leaders
and The Worlds Greatest Fly Fishermen!
Seney Point Resort - Buffalo, Wyoming
Frank Seney 1911-1993
Fred Seney 1911-1991

The 1965 Cessna 210

Buffalo Wyoming Airport

The plane I learned to fly in at 7 years old

Found among the personal flight logs of:

Chuck Yeager
Bell X-1 Program — Edwards Air Force Base
Never published

Just before you break through the sound barrier,
the airplane shakes the most.

That's where a lot of men turn back.
Not because the machine is failing,
but because it's telling them the truth all at once.

Every mark on the dial means something.
Not a dare. A warning.

I learned early that you don't beat an airplane.
You listen to it. You fly it enough to know when it's talking
and when it's just making noise.

When the X-1 went supersonic,
it didn't get rougher.
It got smoother.

The red line wasn't there to stop us.
It was there to tell us who was ready to go on.

Push it without understanding,
and you won't live long enough to learn.
Respect it, and the air will carry you farther than courage ever
could.

At the moment of truth,
there are either reasons
or results. - CY

Chuck Yeager October 14, 1947

Chapter 1

THE HANGAR

The hangar was quiet in the way Kade Vance trusted—no voices, no music, no urgency. Just cooling metal ticking softly and the smell of oil and old aluminum warming in the afternoon sun.

He stood barefoot on the concrete, one sock hooked on a tool cart, rolling a length of safety wire between his fingers. In front of him, a Cessna 210 sat with its cowling open, patient and exposed, the way honest machines always were when you treated them right.

Kade trusted machines.

Not blindly. Instinctively.

Machines didn't lie. They didn't soften the truth to spare your feelings. If something was wrong, they told you—plainly—if you bothered to listen.

He leaned in, checked a torque stripe he'd laid down earlier, then reached for a flashlight even though he already knew what he'd see. Old habit. Old discipline. Wyoming habits didn't fade just because the hangar was closer to the ocean now.

Behind him, Maggie lifted her head from the sun-warmed concrete, yawned, and dropped it back down with a grunt that sounded like mild disapproval. She'd learned early that hangar days meant waiting.

Kade smiled without turning around.

"Almost," he said. He wasn't sure whether he meant the airplane or himself.

He closed the cowling, wiped his hands on a rag older than most tech startups, and stepped back. The hangar looked exactly the way he liked it—tools where he expected them, nothing he didn't recognize, no wasted motion. It wasn't tidy. It was ready.

That mattered.

Outside the hangar door, his 1965 Ford F-250 sat in the sun like a stubborn promise—Frank Vance's old resort truck, faded paint, straight body, still doing its job sixty years later. Kade glanced at it the way you glanced at family: quick, private, grateful.

He cracked a beer from the fridge beside the workbench and sat on an overturned crate. The light had gone soft, slanting in through the open doors, turning dust motes into something almost deliberate.

Kade took a pull, exhaled, and reached for the folded magazine on the bench.

Controller.

He didn't remember subscribing. Aviation had a way of finding its people.

He flipped past glossy spreads of jets built for people who didn't like turbulence and cabins designed to keep pilots insulated from the machines they were supposed to understand. Too much leather. Too much glass. Too much software pretending it knew better.

Then a listing stopped him.

Not because it shouted.

Because it didn't.

A small photo. Clean. Unimpressive. Almost apologetic.

1975 Learjet 25B
Low time. Clean logs. Estate auction.

Kade leaned back, beer forgotten halfway to his mouth.

"Huh."

Old Lears had a reputation.

Pilots talked about them the way mechanics talked about sixties Ferraris—brute power, minimal forgiveness, built before lawyers learned how to fly. They climbed like homesick angels and punished hesitation. No computers. No smoothing. Just thrust, air, and consequences.

They were rude airplanes.

Kade liked rude airplanes.

He scanned the specs. Conservative numbers. Careful language. Whoever wrote the listing either didn't understand what they had—or understood it perfectly and wanted it gone quietly.

Estate sale meant someone had stopped caring.

Low time meant someone once cared a great deal.

Kade's mind did what it always did when a machine caught his attention.

It didn't daydream.

It assessed.

Strip the cabin. Lose the fluff. Expose the structure. Industrial floor. Tie-down rails. A place for a duffel, a rifle case, tools that mattered. Fold-down bunk. A fridge that didn't pretend to be a bar.

Not luxury.

Utility.

A jet you could live out of if you had to.

Paint it matte. No shine. No reflections. Race-plane smooth—the kind of finish you ran your hand over because it felt fast even standing still.

Keep the round gauges. The old needles that moved when something actually changed. Add modern avionics for awareness, not control. Let the airplane talk. Don't drown it out.

He felt the smile before he noticed it.

Maggie lifted her head again, ears pricking like she'd heard the change in his breathing.

"Don't," Kade said. "I'm just thinking."

He read the listing again.

He didn't need another airplane. He especially didn't need a fifty-year-old jet with a reputation for biting the unprepared.

But needing something and wanting it had never been the same thing.

Outside, a jet crossed high overhead, contrail slicing the sky clean and white. Fast enough that no one on the ground felt a thing.

Kade watched it for a moment, then looked back at the hangar, the tools, the quiet—at the old truck and the old airplane and the familiar comfort of things that didn't pretend.

The listing hadn't shown the cockpit.

But Kade already knew what he'd find—round gauges packed tight, engine instruments stacked where you couldn't afford to look away, a windshield that didn't soften anything ahead of you. No buffers. No automation smoothing the edges.

Jets like that didn't shout when something was wrong. They didn't forgive hesitation. They assumed the pilot knew exactly where the line was—and what happened if he crossed it.

And when the moment came, they didn't stop you.

"Yeah," he said softly.
"That could be fun."

RED LINE VIOLATION • The Runway Rogue Series • Book EIGHT

Chapter 2

THE AUCTION

The auction wasn't glamorous, which Kade took as a good sign.

No velvet ropes. No champagne. No influencer energy pretending to understand airplanes. Just a quiet municipal hangar two states inland, folding chairs lined up on a concrete floor, and a handful of men who all looked like they'd rather be somewhere else.

Kade liked those kinds of rooms. They were honest.

The Lear sat off to the side, nose pointed toward the open hangar doors like it was already planning its exit. White paint dulled by time, stainless steel still catching the light where it mattered. No dents. No obvious sins. The kind of airplane that hadn't been loved lately—but hadn't been abused either.

He walked around it slowly, hands in his pockets, not touching anything. There was no need. The jet told its story if you knew how to look.

Straight panels. Tight seams. No oil stains that didn't belong. Tires with honest wear, not panic replacements.

Someone had flown it enough to keep it alive, then stopped before neglect turned into damage.

Estate sale, the listing had said.

That usually meant one of two things:
A widow who wanted it gone.
Or children who didn't understand what it was.

Both made for good buying conditions.

Kade checked the logs at a folding table near the back, flipping pages the way he always did—fast, then slower, then fast again. Engine times were low. Not suspiciously low. Just... reasonable. Maintenance entries were neat. Not over-documented. No nervous over-explaining.

This airplane hadn't been hiding anything.

That was rare.

The auctioneer cleared his throat and started warming up the room with smaller items—ground equipment, spare parts, things that got people nodding without committing. Kade took a seat in the second row, close enough to hear, far enough to watch.

He noticed who else was there.

Two guys who looked like brokers. One kid who'd watched too many YouTube videos. An older man in a blazer who didn't stop checking his phone. No one who looked like they *needed* the Lear.

That mattered.

When the jet finally came up, the room didn't change much. No buzz. No sudden attention. Just the auctioneer's voice echoing lightly off the hangar walls.

"1975 Learjet 25B. Low time. Clean logs. Estate sale. We'll start the bidding at—"

The opening number was lower than Kade expected.

He didn't move.

The kid bid first. Too quickly. The brokers waited, doing math in their heads, already thinking about resale. Kade let the number climb just enough to feel the rhythm, then raised his paddle once.

Clean. Calm. No drama.

The kid hesitated. Bid again. The blazer checked his phone and dropped out. One broker followed, then the other. The kid stalled, eyes flicking back to the jet like it might offer advice.

It didn't.

The auctioneer looked around.

"Going once."

Kade felt the quiet settle.

"Going twice."

The kid shook his head.

"Sold."

The gavel came down with a sound that felt heavier than it should have.

Kade exhaled.

That was it.

No applause. No congratulations. Just paperwork sliding across a folding table and a woman with a clipboard asking for a signature like this happened every day.

Which, for her, it probably did.

For Kade, it didn't really land until he was standing alone again, hand resting on the Lear's nose, the metal cool under his palm.

"Well," he said quietly. "Guess we're doing this."

The seller's representative—a polite man who looked relieved—joined him.

"She's flown regularly," the man said. "Just... not lately."

Kade nodded. "That's usually how it goes."

"You flying her home yourself?"

Kade glanced at the cockpit, then back at the man.

"Yeah."

The man hesitated. "You've flown Lears before?"

Kade smiled—not the kind that answered the question directly.

"I've flown things that tell the truth."

That seemed to satisfy him. Or at least end the conversation.

A few hours later, Kade was strapped into a cockpit that felt like a time capsule. Round gauges. Mechanical switches. No screens pretending to think for him. Just systems that assumed the pilot knew what he was doing—or would learn quickly.

He ran the checklist slowly. Not because he had to. Because the airplane deserved it.

The engines lit with a bark that made him grin despite himself. Thrust came alive fast—eager, almost impatient. The Lear didn't idle politely. It *waited*.

Taxiing out, Kade felt the weight—or lack of it. The jet felt light on its feet, like it wanted to break free from the ground sooner than necessary.

He lined up, took a breath, and advanced the throttles.

Acceleration came hard and clean. No hesitation. No argument. The runway disappeared faster than it should have.

"Okay," Kade said aloud. "I hear you."

The Lear lifted off and climbed like it had somewhere important to be.

Leveling off later, cruising comfortably, Kade settled into the rhythm of the airplane. It didn't feel delicate. It felt *alive*. Responsive. Honest. Slightly offended if you treated it casually.

He glanced at the airspeed, then back out at the sky.

This thing liked to go fast.

Not recklessly. Purposefully.

Kade leaned back, hands light on the controls, listening—not to the engines, not to the gauges, but to the way the airplane moved through the air.

There was nothing strange yet.

Nothing alarming.

Just a feeling he couldn't quite name.

And the quiet realization that flying it home was going to be a lot more interesting than he'd expected.

RED LINE VIOLATION • The Runway Rogue Series • Book EIGHT

Chapter 3

TRIM FOR CRUISE

The Lear liked altitude.

Kade felt it the moment the climb eased and the jet settled into its stride. Engines smoothed out, vibrations softened into something steady and confident, like the airplane had finally stopped tolerating the ground and remembered who it was meant to be.

He trimmed for cruise and let his hands rest lightly on the yoke.

That was always the tell.

When a machine was right, it didn't demand attention. It invited it.

The air was clean up here—thin, cold, uncomplicated. Sunlight poured through the windshield, bleaching the horizon until sky and earth blurred into something simpler than either one alone.

Kade exhaled and let the noise fall away.

This was the part he'd missed.

Not speed.
Not altitude.

The *space*.

There was a moment in every flight—usually once everything was stable, the work done, the systems quiet—when time loosened its grip. When the cockpit stopped being a workplace and became something closer to a confessional.

You could think up here.

You could remember.

The Lear hummed beneath him, content, almost smug. It flew like it had been built by people who assumed the pilot would know what to do next. No warnings. No second-guessing. Just an understanding between man and machine.

Kade glanced at the gauges, then out at the long, empty stretch of sky ahead.

He thought about his grandfather.

Frank Vance had never flown jets. He'd flown fishermen, supplies, the occasional Hollywood type who wanted to say they'd landed somewhere remote. He'd driven trucks instead—big, stubborn ones that smelled like oil and pine sap and work.

The old Ford. Sixty years old now. Still running. Still honest.

Frank used to say machines had personalities. Not souls—he wasn't mystical—but tendencies. You learned them, respected them, and they'd take care of you. Ignore them, and they'd remind you who was in charge.

Kade had learned early which lessons stuck.

He'd learned to drive before most kids learned to read. Learned that speed wasn't dangerous—*inattention* was. Learned that silence didn't mean nothing was happening. It meant you hadn't learned to hear yet.

Those lessons carried.

They carried through bad decisions, worse people, and a life that had taken turns he hadn't planned but somehow never regretted. Through hangars and hotel rooms and jobs that ended with handshakes instead of headlines.

He'd always come back to the same things.

Airplanes that told the truth.
Trucks that started when you needed them.
Work that mattered, even if no one noticed.

The Lear nudged slightly as it crossed an invisible seam in the sky. Kade corrected without thinking, fingers moving more from memory than intention.

He smiled.

This jet was different from the PC-24—less civilized, more direct. And different from the old 210—faster, sharper, less forgiving. It lived somewhere in between, like it hadn't decided what era it belonged to and didn't particularly care.

Kade checked the fuel flow. The numbers looked... better than expected.

He frowned slightly, recalculated, then shrugged.

Old jets. New surprises.

Below him, the land unfolded in broad strokes—fields, rivers, stretches of nothing that went on long enough to make you forget what urgency felt like. From up here, everything looked quieter. Simpler.

He'd always liked that about flying.

Problems flattened out. Noise faded. Perspective returned.

He adjusted the seat, took another sip from his water bottle, and let his thoughts drift.

This was supposed to be fun.

A project.
A distraction.
Something mechanical and manageable.

He hadn't bought the Lear because he needed it. He'd bought it because it felt like something worth understanding.

Kade glanced at the Mach number creeping toward the high end of comfortable cruise.

The Lear didn't complain.

It felt... happier.

That was odd.

Fast airplanes usually got twitchy when you pushed them. Edges sharpened. Controls stiffened. The sky reminded you it was still in charge.

This one didn't.

It smoothed out, like it had finally found the pace it preferred.

Kade eased the throttles back a hair, watching for a reaction.

Nothing.

He pushed them forward again.

The hum deepened, steadied, almost *organized*.

He tilted his head slightly, the way you did when you heard a sound that didn't quite fit.

"That's interesting," he said to the empty cockpit.

The Lear kept flying.

Kade trimmed again, hands light, letting the jet settle where it seemed to want to be.

Whatever this airplane was, it hadn't been built to dawdle.

And for the first time since takeoff, Kade felt a quiet certainty form—not excitement, not concern, just a calm, deliberate awareness.

This trip home was going to give him plenty to think about.

Chapter 4

FLYING IT HOME

The sun was dropping behind him now, stretching the world long and flat beneath the Lear's wings. Late afternoon light turned rivers into molten lines and fields into brushed bronze, the kind of view that made distance feel negotiable.

Kade adjusted the seat, loosened his shoulders, and let the jet do what it clearly wanted to do.

Fly.

The Lear had stopped climbing hours ago. Now it simply *moved*—clean, level, unhurried in the way only fast machines could be. The engines weren't loud so much as present, a steady pressure at his back, like a hand that didn't need to push anymore.

He trimmed again. Out of habit. Out of respect.

The airplane barely noticed.

That was the thing about older machines. When you got them right, they stayed right. No software corrections. No constant negotiation. You set the condition, and they held it.

Kade glanced at the Mach number.

High for a ferry flight. Higher than he usually cruised anything that wasn't on someone else's clock.

The Lear didn't care.

He scanned the gauges again, slower this time. Oil pressure steady. Temps where they belonged. Fuel burn still… lower than it had any right to be.

He frowned, ran the math a second time.

Same answer.

"Okay," he said quietly. "I see you."

Below him, the terrain shifted in broad, unannounced transitions—mountain giving way to plateau, plateau softening into farmland, rivers threading through it all like afterthoughts. From thirty-seven thousand feet, the earth lost its urgency. Patterns mattered more than details.

That's when he felt it.

Not turbulence.

Not vibration.

Something subtler.

A change in the *texture* of the airframe beneath him.

It wasn't a shake. It was a hum—low, even, almost pleasant. The kind of sound you felt more than heard, traveling up through the seat rails and into his spine.

Kade stiffened slightly, hands lightening on the controls.

He waited.

Nothing else changed. No warning lights. No deviation in pitch or yaw. The Lear flew on, unbothered, perfectly content.

The hum faded as gradually as it had arrived.

Kade exhaled, realizing he'd been holding his breath.

"Probably just you settling in," he muttered, though he wasn't convinced.

He watched the land scroll beneath him, then felt it again.

This time shorter. Sharper.

Different.

He glanced down. The aircraft was passing over a wide lake now, sunlight breaking across the surface in fractured reflections. The hum softened—almost dissolved—like someone had turned down the volume.

Kade's brow creased.

The moment the shoreline slipped behind him and dry land returned, the sensation came back. Firmer. More structured.

He shifted slightly in the seat, listening with his whole body now.

"That's…" He paused, searching for the word. "Odd."

Pilots learned early not to chase ghosts. Airplanes made noises. Air did strange things. You noted it, logged it, and moved on unless it demanded more.

This didn't demand anything.

It just… repeated.

Kade eased the throttles back a fraction.

The hum loosened, lost cohesion.

He advanced them again.

It returned.

Stronger.

He didn't smile.

He didn't frown.

He simply *noticed*.

The Mach number edged higher, settling just under where he'd normally stop without thinking about it. The Lear felt better there—smoother, calmer, almost balanced in a way it hadn't been ten knots slower.

Fast airplanes weren't supposed to do that.

They were supposed to get twitchy. Sharp. Demanding.

This one felt like it had found its stride.

Kade leaned back, eyes forward, senses stretched.

Below him now: farmland. Soft land. Worked land. Roads cut in clean lines, irrigation arcs faintly visible like fingerprints.

The hum changed again.

Not louder.

Different.

Less rigid. Less precise.

Kade's heartbeat ticked up a notch.

"Okay," he said softly. "Now you've got my attention."

He reached down and adjusted the seat slightly, feeling for the vibration with deliberate intent. Over fields, it scattered. Over rivers, it thinned. Over a stretch of untouched prairie, it came back tight and steady, almost resonant.

Like a note held in tune.

Kade's mind didn't jump to conclusions.

It cataloged.

He marked the location mentally. Watched the timing. Noted the transition points.

This wasn't random.

That thought settled in quietly, without ceremony.

He wasn't uncomfortable.

He wasn't excited.

He was alert.

The Lear flew on, untroubled, as if nothing unusual was happening at all.

Kade checked the clock. Plenty of daylight left. Plenty of fuel. No reason to rush.

He didn't push the jet harder.

He didn't pull back.

He let it sit exactly where it seemed happiest.

The hum stabilized into something consistent enough that his body adjusted to it, the way you adjusted to a road surface after a few miles. It became part of the environment—noticeable only when it changed.

And it *did* change.

Every time the ground did.

Kade felt a slow grin threaten the edge of his focus and shut it down immediately.

Curiosity was fine.

Assumptions were not.

He flew on, letting the Lear teach him its language one sentence at a time.

By the time the sun dipped lower and the horizon began to soften into dusk, Kade had stopped trying to explain what he was feeling.

He was too busy listening.

Whatever this airplane was doing, it wasn't complaining.

It wasn't protesting.

It wasn't warning him off.

It was behaving exactly the way it had all afternoon—like it had been built for this kind of flight and was mildly surprised it had taken someone this long to let it stretch out.

Kade trimmed once more, hands light, letting the Lear settle where it wanted to live.

"This," he said quietly, almost to himself, "is going to be interesting."

The jet held steady, the hum deep and even, the world sliding beneath them in quiet, unreadable patterns.

And for the first time since the wheels had left the ground, Kade had the unmistakable feeling that flying it home wasn't just a ferry flight anymore.

It was a conversation.

Chapter 5

THE STRIP-DOWN

The hangar smelled different after midnight.

Less sun. More oil. Cold aluminum and dust that had settled into long-term decisions. The kind of smell that said nothing was moving unless you made it move.

Kade liked that hour best.

The Lear rolled in quiet, engines ticking as they cooled, white paint dulled by age under the hangar lights, stainless trim still catching where it mattered. He shut the doors himself, the echo rolling across concrete like punctuation.

Maggie circled twice and claimed her spot near the workbench, tail thumping once in approval. She'd decided the jet was staying.

Kade set the flight bag down, didn't bother unloading it yet. Instead, he stood there for a moment, looking at the airplane the way you looked at something you'd just brought home and hadn't figured out where it belonged yet.

"Alright," he said. "Let's see what you're hiding."

He started with the cabin.

Seats came out first. Heavy. Overbuilt. Designed to reassure passengers who didn't want to know what was happening outside the windows. He unbolted them methodically, stacking hardware in labeled trays, setting the leather aside without ceremony.

Comfort weighed more than most people thought.

The side panels followed. Then the carpet. Then the insulation—thick, yellowed, doing its best to smother every honest vibration the airframe wanted to pass along.

Kade peeled it back and paused.

The airplane felt different already.

Not louder. Not quieter.

More *present*.

Good.

By the time he stopped, the Lear looked less like a corporate jet and more like a machine again—frames and ribs and wiring runs visible, structure doing what structure was meant to do.

He wiped sweat from his forearm and leaned against the bulkhead, breathing slow.

This was the part he liked.

Not the buying.
Not the flying.

The *understanding*.

He walked the length of the cabin, tapping here and there, listening to how the sound changed. Solid spots. Resonant ones. Places that wanted reinforcement. Places that wanted to be left alone.

The jet answered in small ways—different echoes, different tones—like it appreciated being asked instead of told.

Kade sketched ideas on the whiteboard bolted to the hangar wall.

Industrial floor.
Tie-down rails.
Fold-down bunk against the port side.
Gun safe forward, bolted into structure.
Fridge aft—simple, mechanical, no touchscreen nonsense.

A flying RV.

Something you could live out of if plans went sideways.

He wasn't building luxury.

He was building *optionality*.

Hours passed. Tools moved. Music stayed off. The only sounds were the scrape of aluminum, the click of fasteners, the occasional grunt when something came loose that didn't want to.

Around two a.m., he stepped back again.

The Lear looked lighter.

Not physically yet—but mentally. Like it had stopped pretending to be something it wasn't.

He ran a hand along the exposed skin, feeling the smoothness where panels met. Old jets were overbuilt, but they weren't sloppy. Whoever had assembled this one had known what mattered.

Kade smiled faintly.

"Yeah," he said. "I get it now."

He moved to the cockpit.

The analog gauges stared back at him, unapologetic. No menus. No modes. Just needles and numbers and truth.

He made a note to keep them.

Add modern avionics, sure—but quietly. Awareness without interference. Information without argument.

The thought drifted back to the flight.

The hum.
The way it had changed over water. Over fields. Over untouched ground.

He stopped himself.

Not yet.

First things first.

He stepped outside the hangar for air. The night was cool, quiet. The old Ford sat where it always did, paint faded, body straight. Frank's truck.

Frank's rules.

Fix it right.
Don't rush.
Listen before you decide.

Kade leaned against the fender, looked back at the Lear through the open doors.

He hadn't bought it because he needed speed.

He'd bought it because it felt like a machine that still had something to say.

And now that he'd started stripping away the noise, it was getting easier to hear.

Chapter 6

HOT-ROD LOGIC

Speed wasn't the goal.

It never was.

Speed was a *result*.

Kade had learned that early—long before jets, long before runways. Speed came when friction was removed, not when power was added. Anyone could shove more fuel into something. Not everyone knew what to shave away.

He stood beneath the Lear's wing with a flashlight, running the beam along the skin where panels met. Old jets wore their seams openly. They hadn't been built to hide anything.

Which meant you could improve them.

He wasn't looking for records. He was looking for *honesty*.

Weight came first.

Anything that didn't contribute to structure, safety, or purpose was suspect. Soundproofing. Decorative panels. Redundant brackets that existed because someone once had a bad meeting with a lawyer.

Gone.

Then drag.

The Lear wasn't sleek by modern standards, but it was clean—cleaner than people remembered. The trick was letting it stay that way.

Flush fasteners where they mattered.
Sealant where airflow told him it wanted it.
Polish where friction whispered instead of shouted.

He worked the way he always did—slow, methodical, listening.

He thought about engines.

The originals were good. Overpowered for their time. Brutal when mishandled. But there were options now—materials, tolerances, updates that didn't change the soul of the machine.

He wasn't building a monster.

He was *finishing an idea*.

Avionics came next on the board.

Keep the round gauges. Keep the needles that moved when something real changed. Add a modern Garmin stack for situational awareness—not control. The jet flew just fine without being told what it felt like.

Information was helpful.

Interference was not.

By mid-morning, the hangar floor was littered with evidence of progress—parts laid out cleanly, notes taped to bulkheads, measurements scribbled in a notebook that looked older than some pilots he knew.

Kade stepped back and looked at the airplane again.

White. Plain. Anonymous.

For now.

Paint would come later. After the math. After the intent was locked in. Paint was a statement, and he wasn't ready to make it yet.

He ran the numbers again.

Thrust-to-weight was better than it had any right to be.

Drag was going down.

The margins were opening up.

Not dangerously.

Comfortably.

That was the thing that kept nagging at him.

Fast airplanes were supposed to feel sharp at the edges. Like they were reminding you not to get greedy. This one felt like it was inviting him to stay a little longer.

He thought about the ferry flight again. The way the jet had smoothed out as it went faster. The way the hum had organized itself, like something finding a frequency it liked.

Kade didn't label it.

He didn't speculate.

He just wrote it down.

Because patterns didn't announce themselves.

They waited to be noticed.

He capped the marker, stepped back, and nodded once.

"Alright," he said to the empty hangar. "Let's see what happens when we do it again."

Chapter 7

THE SECOND RUN

The second flight was never about curiosity.

Curiosity had already been satisfied.

This one was about discipline.

Kade stood alone on the ramp just after dawn, the world still undecided about waking up. The Lear sat exactly where he'd left it, white paint catching the pale light, stainless trim dull and honest. No one else around. No fuel trucks yet. No line guys. Just him, the airplane, and the quiet that came before people complicated things.

He liked it this way.

The first flight home could be dismissed as anything—fatigue, unfamiliarity, coincidence. A pilot adjusting to an old jet. A machine settling into new hands.

The second flight removed excuses.

He walked around the Lear slowly, touching nothing, seeing everything. Tires. Panels. Control surfaces. The seams he'd cleaned and sealed the night before. The places he'd deliberately left alone.

Everything where it belonged.

Maggie watched from the hangar door, head tilted, as if evaluating whether this counted as routine or adventure. She'd learned the difference.

"This one's quick," Kade said quietly. "You stay."

She snorted and turned back to her blanket.

Preflight took longer than it needed to. Not because anything was wrong—but because Kade didn't rush airplanes that were trying to tell him something.

He ran his hand along the fuselage, felt the temperature difference between shaded aluminum and sunlit metal. Old habit. Old instinct. Machines expanded and contracted whether you noticed or not. You could work with that—or ignore it and let it surprise you later.

The cockpit smelled faintly different now. Less upholstery. More machine. Exposed structure carried sound differently, sharper, more immediate. He liked that.

Engines lit clean. Not eager. Not reluctant. Just ready.

Taxi was uneventful, which was exactly what he wanted. No wandering gauges. No minor annoyances trying to earn attention.

He lined up, advanced the throttles smoothly, and felt the Lear surge forward with the same rude enthusiasm as the day before. Acceleration pressed him back—not violently, but insistently. This airplane did not tolerate indecision.

Rotation came early. Climb aggressive. The Lear ate altitude like it had been offended by the ground.

Kade let it.

He leveled off higher this time. Gave himself room. Gave the airplane space to breathe.

The sky ahead was empty. No traffic conflicts. No reason to explain anything to anyone. Just a long, straight line of air and time.

That was intentional.

He trimmed for cruise and sat back, hands light, letting the jet settle.

This time, he wasn't distracted by novelty. He wasn't reminiscing. He wasn't daydreaming.

He was listening.

The Lear stabilized quickly, engines smoothing into that deep, even pressure that felt less like sound and more like presence. The airplane felt... balanced. Like it had reached a condition it preferred.

Kade watched the Mach number rise, not pushing, not pulling—just allowing.

The hum came back sooner this time.

It didn't surprise him.

It arrived gently, almost politely, threading up through the seat and into his spine like a low note struck on a string instrument. The vibration wasn't random. It had structure. Rhythm.

Kade didn't move.

He waited.

Below him, the terrain shifted from foothills into a wide basin, land still rough and unworked, colors muted by early light. The hum tightened.

There it is.

He glanced at the clock. Noted the time. Noted the position.

No reaction from the jet. No deviation in attitude. No change in fuel flow. Everything else remained perfectly ordinary.

Which made the extraordinary part harder to ignore.

The land below transitioned again—this time into irrigated fields, precise arcs of green etched into brown. The hum loosened. Lost cohesion. Not gone, just… scattered.

Kade adjusted the throttles back a hair.

The vibration softened.

Forward again.

It returned.

Not stronger—*cleaner*.

He didn't smile.

He wrote it down.

Mental notes first. Physical notes later.

The lake came next. Broad and reflective, surface broken only by wind. As the Lear crossed the shoreline, the hum thinned almost to nothing. The airplane felt smoother still—but quieter in the wrong way, like something had stopped answering.

Kade felt a flicker of satisfaction.

Patterns were comforting.

Mysteries were not.

He waited until dry land returned.

The vibration came back immediately, sharper than before. Not louder—more precise. As if the airplane had found a channel and locked onto it.

Kade's breathing slowed.

This was no longer interesting.

This was *repeatable.*

He reached down and adjusted the seat slightly, not for comfort but for feedback. The exposed structure transmitted more now, the absence of insulation making the Lear more honest than it had been in decades.

The hum changed again as the jet passed over a long stretch of untouched prairie. No roads. No irrigation. No development. Just land that had never been rearranged.

The vibration steadied into something almost musical. A held note. Pure. Resonant.

Kade closed his eyes for half a second—not long enough to lose anything, just long enough to feel it without interpretation.

The airplane was doing exactly what it had done yesterday.

The ground was answering the same way.

He opened his eyes.

"Okay," he said quietly. "Now we're talking."

He resisted the urge to push harder. That was the trick. Curiosity wanted escalation. Discipline demanded restraint.

You didn't scare animals you wanted to study.

You didn't startle machines that were showing you something for free.

He held speed. Held altitude. Held heading.

The Lear stayed there with him, content, cooperative, like it had been waiting for someone patient enough to stop asking it to perform.

Minutes passed.

The hum did not drift. Did not degrade. Did not wander.

It stayed locked in, as stable as a well-trimmed prop.

Kade's mind shifted gears.

Not speculation.

Correlation.

He tracked transitions. Watched how long the vibration took to change after terrain shifts. Counted seconds between shoreline crossings and sensation changes. Noted how quickly it stabilized over homogeneous ground.

This wasn't magic.

It was response.

Something was coupling. Something was interacting.

He didn't know what.

Yet.

The Mach number crept higher on its own, settling just under where he'd normally rein it in without thinking.

The Lear felt better there.

Calmer.

Balanced.

That was the part that bothered him.

Fast airplanes weren't supposed to relax as they approached the edge of their envelope. They were supposed to demand more attention, not less.

This one felt like it had found its natural pace.

Kade's heartbeat stayed steady, but something behind his eyes sharpened.

He was no longer alone in the cockpit.

Not literally.

But conceptually.

The airplane wasn't just flying.

It was *participating*.

The land below changed again—this time into rolling hills, denser geology, older rock. The hum shifted subtly, picking up a second layer, like an overtone riding above the base frequency.

Kade sat up a fraction.

That was new.

He adjusted power slightly. The overtone faded. Returned when he brought it back.

He swallowed.

"Alright," he said, more firmly now. "That's enough for today."

He didn't want first discoveries to turn into last mistakes.

He eased the throttles back, watching the Mach number fall. The vibration loosened, unraveled, disappeared—not abruptly, but reluctantly, like a conversation ending mid-thought.

The Lear remained smooth. Cooperative. Innocent.

He turned back toward home, letting the jet drift into a more conservative cruise. The sky ahead looked the same as it had an hour ago.

Kade knew better.

On descent, nothing unusual happened. The hum didn't return. The airplane behaved like every other fast jet in the world.

Which somehow made everything worse.

The landing was uneventful. Rollout clean. Taxi quiet.

Back in the hangar, engines ticking down, Kade sat in the cockpit longer than necessary, hands resting on his thighs, eyes unfocused.

He wasn't shaken.

He wasn't thrilled.

He was... oriented.

The kind of orientation you felt when a map finally matched the ground beneath your feet.

He shut down, climbed out, and stood on the hangar floor looking at the Lear like it had just revealed a second face.

"Alright," he said again, this time without humor. "I hear you."

Maggie trotted over, sniffed the tire, and sat.

Kade didn't move.

He knew what came next.

Not another flight.

Not yet.

First, he needed numbers. Context. A second set of eyes that didn't get distracted by romance or fear.

He reached for his phone.

Scrolled once.

Stopped.

Zara's name sat there, exactly where he expected it to be.

He didn't call.

Not yet.

He looked back at the airplane, white and unremarkable, giving nothing away.

This wasn't a fluke.

This wasn't turbulence.

This wasn't imagination.

Whatever the Lear was doing, it had done it twice now, in the same way, over the same kinds of ground.

That made it real.

Kade pocketed the phone and reached for his notebook instead.

He wrote one line, carefully.

Repeatable at speed. Terrain dependent.

Then he closed the notebook.

Tomorrow, he'd do it again.

And after that—

He glanced once more at the Lear, at the exposed cabin, the honest gauges, the old bones doing something new.

After that, he'd bring someone else into the conversation.

Chapter 8

MACH .92

Kade didn't plan the number.

That was the thing that stuck with him later.

Mach point nine two wasn't a target. It wasn't a challenge. It wasn't even a decision in the way pilots usually meant decisions. It was simply where the Lear wanted to live when everything else was right.

He took off just after noon, the sky scrubbed clean by a high-pressure system that made the horizon look farther away than it should have. Visibility stretched forever. The kind of day that made pilots cocky if they weren't careful.

Kade wasn't.

He climbed higher than the day before. Not because he needed to—but because he wanted fewer variables. Less weather. Less noise. Less chance that something unrelated would blur the signal he was trying not to chase too hard.

The Lear climbed eagerly, engines breathing easier as the air thinned. He leveled at forty-one thousand, trimmed carefully, and let the jet settle into its rhythm.

No rush.

He didn't touch the throttles right away.

Instead, he flew for nearly twenty minutes at a conservative cruise, letting the airplane normalize, letting himself normalize with it. He watched fuel flow stabilize. Watched temperatures settle into the narrow band that told him everything was content.

Then he nudged the throttles forward.

Not much.

The Mach number responded slowly at first, easing upward the way it always did. The Lear didn't surge. Didn't complain. It simply leaned into the push, smooth and confident, like it had been waiting for permission.

Mach .85.

The hum appeared almost immediately.

Kade felt it before he acknowledged it—a low, coherent vibration threading through the seat rails and into his spine. Not uncomfortable. Not distracting.

Familiar.

He nodded once, more to himself than the airplane.

"Alright," he said quietly. "Same song."

He held it there, watching the land pass beneath him. The terrain today was different—more rock, less water—but the behavior was the same. The vibration tightened over dense ground, loosened over softer stretches.

It was consistent enough now that his body stopped reacting to it.

Which was dangerous.

Kade eased the throttles forward again.

Mach .88.

The Lear felt better.

That was the part he still couldn't reconcile.

Fast airplanes got sharp as you approached their limits. Controls stiffened. Margins narrowed. They reminded you, politely or otherwise, that physics was not a negotiation.

This one did the opposite.

It smoothed out.

The vibration didn't increase. It clarified.

The hum organized itself into something almost geometric, as if the airplane had locked into a frequency it preferred—one that made everything else simpler instead of more complicated.

Kade swallowed.

"Okay," he said. "That's new."

He glanced at the Mach tape as it edged upward again, settling at .90 without any additional input. The Lear wasn't accelerating aggressively. It was... drifting. Like a boat finding a current.

Kade tightened his focus.

This was no longer about sensation.

This was about limits.

Mach .91.

The sky outside the windshield looked unchanged. No shock waves. No condensation. No visual cues that anything significant was happening.

Inside the cockpit, though, the airplane felt different.

Not strained.

Aligned.

The vibration deepened—not louder, not harsher—but more present, like a standing wave that had finally stopped wandering. It felt less like movement and more like pressure.

Kade shifted in his seat, testing the feedback.

The hum was strongest now. Stable. Persistent. As if the Lear had crossed an invisible threshold and decided to stay there.

Mach .92.

The number settled and didn't move.

Kade hadn't pushed it there.

It had arrived.

He held his breath without realizing it.

The hum changed again.

Not in amplitude—but in *texture*.

It spread.

Instead of being localized to the seat and lower frame, it seemed to fill the cockpit, subtle vibrations riding the structure itself. Not rattling. Not shaking.

Resonating.

Kade's scalp prickled.

This wasn't turbulence.

This wasn't airflow.

This was something coupling through the airframe in a way he'd never felt before—not in jets, not in turboprops, not even in helicopters where vibration was a given.

The Lear felt... tuned.

"Jesus," he murmured.

He checked the gauges again. Everything was green. Better than green. Temperatures were lower than expected. Fuel flow steady. Pressurization smooth.

The airplane wasn't under stress.

If anything, it seemed relieved.

The land below was a wide stretch of ancient terrain—hard rock, old formations, no agriculture, no water to speak of. The hum intensified, becoming almost *focused*, like a beam that had snapped into alignment.

Kade's mind raced—not with theories, but with consequences.

If this was real…

If this was consistent…

He eased the throttles back a fraction.

Mach .91.

The vibration loosened slightly. Lost some cohesion.

Forward again.

Mach .92.

It snapped back.

Hard.

Kade felt it in his teeth.

"Holy hell," he whispered.

He didn't push further.

That was the line.

Not because he was afraid of what lay beyond it—but because he understood something fundamental had just revealed itself, and you didn't trample revelations by demanding more before you understood what you'd been given.

Mach .92 wasn't just a speed.

It was a condition.

He held it there for nearly ten minutes.

The Lear flew like it was on rails. Controls light. Stable. No tendency to diverge. No creeping instability.

The vibration stayed locked in, unwavering, as long as the ground below remained geologically consistent. When the terrain changed—softened, fractured, watered—the hum degraded, blurred, then sharpened again as the land hardened.

Kade stared straight ahead, pulse steady but elevated, the way it got when a truth settled in that you couldn't unsee.

This wasn't random.

This wasn't noise.

This was *interaction*.

He didn't know the mechanism yet. Didn't need to.

The implications were already forming, uninvited.

Mapping.

Penetration.

Subsurface response.

He backed out of the speed slowly, watching the Mach number slide down through .90, .88, .85. The vibration unwound reluctantly, like something being asked to stop mid-sentence.

By the time he reached a conservative cruise again, the Lear felt ordinary.

Too ordinary.

He exhaled for the first time in minutes.

"Okay," he said. "That's enough."

The rest of the flight passed without incident. No anomalies. No hum. No sense of alignment.

Just a fast jet flying through empty sky.

Which somehow felt wrong now.

Back on the ground, Kade shut down and sat in the cockpit longer than usual, hands resting on his knees, the hum still echoing faintly in his memory like a phantom sensation.

Mach .92.

He wrote it down immediately, before memory could soften it.

Mach .92 — threshold. Resonance locks. Terrain dependent. Repeatable.

He stared at the words.

That wasn't a note.

It was a line in the sand.

Kade climbed out, closed the door, and stood on the hangar floor staring at the Lear as if it might speak again.

White paint. Old jet. No outward sign of what it had just done.

That was the dangerous part.

He walked outside, leaned against Frank's old truck, and looked up at the sky. Jets passed high overhead, unaware, moving fast enough to be impressive but slow enough to remain harmless.

On purpose.

Kade felt the pieces begin to align—not fully, not cleanly—but enough to make him uneasy.

Speed limits.
Noise rules.
Why overland supersonic flight had been frozen in time.

Not because of sound.

Because of *what sound could do*.

He didn't jump to conclusions.

But he knew one thing with absolute clarity.

This wasn't just his discovery.

It was something someone, somewhere, had already noticed once—and decided to bury.

Kade reached into his pocket and pulled out his phone.

This time, he didn't hesitate.

He scrolled once.

Tapped.

"Zara," he said when she answered, voice calm despite the storm behind it. "I need you in the hangar. And I need you to bring everything you know about ultrasound, resonance, and subsurface imaging."

There was a pause on the line.

"Okay," she said carefully. "How much trouble are we talking about?"

Kade looked back at the Lear.

"At least Mach .92 worth," he said.

He ended the call and stood there a moment longer, listening to the quiet.

The sound barrier hadn't been broken today.

It had been *tuned*.

And nothing about that felt accidental.

Chapter 9

ZARA

Zara Quinn didn't ask what time it was.

That alone told Kade she was already awake—and probably halfway through figuring out why he'd called.

She showed up at the hangar just after sunset, a compact electric SUV rolling quietly onto the apron like it didn't want to announce itself. No rush. No lights blazing. Just purposeful movement, the kind that assumed it belonged wherever it stopped.

Kade watched from inside as she stepped out, jacket slung over one shoulder, tablet tucked under her arm. She paused for half a second, eyes scanning the hangar, the Lear, the old Ford parked outside like a relic that refused to die.

Then she smiled.

"That's new," she said when she walked in.

"Bought it on a whim," Kade replied. "Fifty years old. Bad attitude."

Zara nodded approvingly. "My favorite kind of machine."

She didn't hug him. Didn't ask how he was. Didn't ask what he needed.

She walked straight to the Lear.

Up close, she took it in the way engineers and chess players did—holistically. Not admiring the lines so much as *reading* them. White paint dulled by age. Exposed cabin through the open door. Analog cockpit unapologetically staring back.

"This thing shouldn't feel fast sitting still," she said.

"But it does," Kade replied.

She glanced back at him. "Yeah. It does."

Zara Quinn wasn't impressed easily. She'd grown up around systems that bent rules quietly—networks, algorithms, information flows that behaved one way on paper and another way in the real world. She trusted patterns more than credentials, anomalies more than explanations.

Which was why Kade had called her.

She stepped into the cabin, eyes adjusting quickly to the stripped-down interior. No insulation. Bare ribs. Structure doing exactly what it had been designed to do.

"You gutted it," she said.

"Listening experiment," Kade replied.

She looked at him now, fully. "That's not a joke, is it?"

"No."

She nodded once and sat on a fold-down crate Kade had repurposed as a work seat. Pulled the tablet out. Didn't turn it on yet.

"Start from the beginning," she said. "But don't explain. Just tell me what you *felt*."

Kade leaned against the bulkhead, arms crossed.

"Speed-dependent vibration," he said. "Consistent. Repeatable. Changes with terrain. Disappears over water. Locks in at Mach point nine two."

Zara didn't interrupt.

"It's not turbulence. Not buffet. Not flutter. It's... organized. Like the airplane finds a frequency it likes and the ground starts answering back."

She tilted her head slightly.

"Answering how?"

Kade hesitated.

"Different ground feels different. Soft land scatters it. Hard land tightens it. Old rock resonates longer. I don't have the words yet."

Zara smiled faintly. "Good. That means you're not forcing them."

She finally turned on the tablet.

"Mach point nine two," she repeated. "That's interesting."

"Because—?"

"Because that's where a lot of things get weird," she said calmly. "Not just aerodynamically."

She tapped the screen, pulling up a blank canvas.

"At subsonic speeds, pressure waves propagate forward. At supersonic, they trail. But near transonic... they *stack*."

Kade watched her hands move—quick, confident, mapping ideas without overcommitting to any of them.

"Energy doesn't disappear," she continued. "It reorganizes. You get compression zones, interference patterns. Standing waves."

She paused, looking up at him.

"And standing waves don't care what medium they're in—as long as something can carry them."

Kade felt a quiet click behind his eyes.

"You're saying the airplane isn't just moving through air."

"I'm saying the airplane might be *coupling* air to something else."

She gestured downward.

"The ground."

Silence stretched.

Maggie shifted near the door, nails clicking once against the concrete.

Zara looked back at the Lear, eyes sharper now.

"Do you have any recordings?" she asked.

"Only subjective," Kade said. "Seat-of-the-pants."

She smiled wider this time. "That's not a weakness. That's how most real discoveries start."

She stood and walked the cabin again, fingertips brushing the exposed structure.

"You stripped the insulation," she said. "That matters. Most aircraft are designed to *hide* vibration, not reveal it."

Kade nodded. "I wanted honesty."

"And you got it," Zara said. "Probably by accident."

She stopped near the cockpit, staring at the gauges.

"This jet was designed before anyone worried about filtering data," she continued. "No fly-by-wire. No software smoothing. It's raw input straight to the pilot."

She turned back to him.

"Kade... this thing is a sensor."

He didn't answer.

Didn't need to.

She was already ahead of him now, eyes lit with that particular focus he'd seen only a few times—when Zara crossed from curiosity into inevitability.

"Ultrasound works by sending energy into tissue and reading what comes back," she said. "Seismic surveys do the same thing with the earth—just slower, louder, messier."

Her fingers moved again, sketching invisible diagrams in the air.

"You might have stumbled into a coupling regime where the aircraft's pressure waves act like a moving excitation source. At the right speed, the right altitude, the right frequency... the ground responds."

Kade swallowed.

"You're talking about imaging."

Zara nodded.

"Not directly," she said. "Not yet. But data. Signals. Enough for reconstruction."

She looked almost reverent now.

"If you can correlate vibration patterns with terrain types... if you can spatially resolve them..."

She stopped herself, exhaled slowly.

"This would be seismic without the trucks. Without the explosions. Without anyone knowing you were doing it."

The hangar felt smaller.

Kade glanced at the closed doors, suddenly aware of how thin aluminum walls really were.

"Who would care?" he asked carefully.

Zara didn't answer right away.

Instead, she pulled up a timeline on her tablet—aviation milestones, regulatory inflection points, things most people never bothered connecting.

"You know why supersonic flight over land was banned?" she asked.

"Sonic booms," Kade said automatically.

She shook her head.

"That's the public reason."

She zoomed in on the late 1950s. Early '60s. Experimental programs. Test pilots. Redacted memos.

"Supersonic pressure waves do more than make noise," she said. "They *interact*. With structures. With geology. With things underground that don't like being noticed."

She looked up at him.

"Imagine discovering, accidentally, that flying fast enough could reveal what was buried."

Kade's jaw tightened.

"Oil," he said.

"Oil," Zara agreed. "Minerals. Tunnels. Facilities. Entire subsurface architectures."

She hesitated, then added quietly:

"Or things that were never meant to be mapped."

The Lear sat silently between them.

Fifty years old. White paint. No markings. No idea what it had just done to history.

Kade leaned back against the bulkhead, arms folded, the weight of it settling in.

"So what do we do?" he asked.

Zara met his gaze.

"We don't tell anyone yet," she said. "We verify. We instrument. We build a model so clean and undeniable that when it finally comes out…"

She smiled, but there was steel behind it.

"…no one can put it back in the ground."

Kade looked at the Lear again, really looked at it.

A hot-rod jet.
A flying RV.
A sensor platform masquerading as nostalgia.

"Mach point nine two," he said.

Zara nodded.

"The sound barrier was never the problem," she said. "It was the *mirror*."

They stood there together in the hangar, the airplane cooling quietly, the world outside unaware that something old had just been seen in a completely new way.

And far above them, jets crossed the sky at carefully approved speeds—fast enough to impress, slow enough to stay blind.

For now.

Chapter 10

THE FIRST MODEL

Zara didn't sleep.

Kade knew that without asking.

By the time he poured the second cup of coffee, she'd already turned the hangar into something that felt less like a workspace and more like a temporary command center. Cables snaked across the concrete. Tablets and laptops sat open on folding tables. A portable server rack hummed quietly near the wall, lights blinking with the kind of patience only machines had.

The Lear sat in the middle of it all, stripped, white, anonymous—its exposed ribs catching the morning light like a skeleton that had decided not to hide anymore.

"This isn't data yet," Zara said, fingers moving across a screen. "It's sensation. Memory. Correlation. Which is still better than most discoveries get."

Kade leaned against the workbench, watching her work.

"What do you need?" he asked.

She didn't look up. "Repeatability."

"You've got that."

She nodded. "Resolution."

That made him smile.

"Figures."

Zara finally looked at him then—eyes sharp, alert, already a few steps ahead.

"Tell me exactly where you were when it locked," she said. "Not generally. Not 'over land.' I want altitude, speed, heading, time, and what the ground looked like before you ever thought about geology."

Kade closed his eyes for a moment—not to remember, but to *re-enter* the flight.

"Forty-one thousand," he said. "Mach .92. Heading east-southeast. Old terrain. Hard rock. No irrigation. No rivers nearby."

She started typing again.

"And the onset?" she asked.

"Clean," Kade said. "No ramp-up. It snaps in when the conditions align."

Zara paused.

"Snaps," she repeated.

"Yeah."

She nodded slowly. "Standing wave behavior."

She pulled up a crude three-dimensional grid on one of the screens—nothing detailed, just a skeletal framework floating in digital space.

"We're not going to model the earth," she said. "That's impossible at this scale."

"Then what are we modeling?"

She finally smiled.

"The interaction."

Her fingers moved faster now, sketching vectors, layering assumptions without locking any of them down.

"Think of the airplane as a moving excitation source," she continued. "At most speeds, the energy dissipates. At Mach .92, the pressure waves organize instead of collapsing. They don't just trail or scatter—they *couple*."

Kade watched the grid begin to pulse faintly.

"With the ground," he said.

"With whatever the ground allows," Zara replied. "Density. Elasticity. Layering. Old rock behaves differently than soft soil. Water absorbs. Air pockets distort. Structures reflect."

She paused again, letting that one land.

"Subsurface structures reflect," she said.

The word *structures* echoed longer than it should have.

Kade folded his arms.

"So this thing," he said, nodding toward the Lear, "isn't imaging like radar."

"No," Zara said. "It's interrogating."

She brought up another display—raw vibration traces she'd started mapping based on Kade's descriptions. Nothing precise yet. Just waveforms stacked against terrain profiles.

"At this stage, all we can do is correlate," she said. "But correlation becomes prediction surprisingly fast once you stop pretending noise is random."

She dragged a slider.

The waveforms tightened.

Another slider.

They loosened.

Zara leaned back slightly, eyes narrowing.

"This is what you felt," she said. "Not sound. Not vibration. *Coherence*."

Kade felt a chill he didn't bother hiding.

"So what happens if we record it properly?" he asked.

Zara didn't answer immediately.

Instead, she stood and walked into the Lear's cabin, hand resting briefly on the exposed frame. She closed her eyes—not theatrically, just enough to feel the machine.

"We turn it into a platform," she said finally. "Not a jet. Not a vehicle. A moving boundary condition."

Kade raised an eyebrow.

"That sounds expensive."

She smiled faintly. "Not compared to what it replaces."

She moved back to the table and pulled up another schematic—this one more refined. Sensor placements. Mounting points. Isolation strategies.

"We don't need fancy hardware," she continued. "Accelerometers. Strain gauges. Pressure transducers. Off-the-shelf stuff. What matters is placement and synchronization."

Kade studied the diagram.

"And AI?" he asked.

Zara nodded. "Eventually. Pattern recognition. Inversion models. We feed it ground truth slowly, carefully."

"Oil logs," Kade said.

"Geological surveys," Zara agreed. "Known formations. Places where we already know what's underground."

She stopped herself, then added quietly:

"And places where we don't."

The hangar hummed softly around them.

Kade felt the weight shift—not heavier, just more defined.

"How fast does this get big?" he asked.

Zara looked at him, really looked at him now.

"The moment it works even once," she said. "It's already too big."

She tapped the screen, freezing the crude model in place.

"This," she said, "is the kind of thing that gets classified retroactively."

Kade exhaled slowly.

"Someone's going to notice."

"Yes," Zara said. "Eventually."

"When?"

She shrugged. "Depends how careful we are."

Silence settled again.

Kade glanced at the Lear, then at the old Ford outside, then back at the glowing screens.

"This started because I wanted a hot rod," he said.

Zara smiled. "That's how most revolutions start. Someone tinkering."

She saved the file, naming it simply:

M092_v1

The cursor blinked beside it, waiting.

"That's not a model yet," she said. "It's a hypothesis."

Kade nodded.

"And hypotheses get tested."

Zara met his gaze.

"In private," she said. "At first."

Kade straightened, decision settling in with the same quiet certainty he felt when trimming an airplane just right.

"Alright," he said. "We fly again."

Zara closed the laptop.

"No," she said gently. "We don't."

He frowned.

She smiled, but there was no humor in it.

"Not yet," she clarified. "First, we build the ears."

She looked back at the Lear—white, old, unassuming.

"Then," she said, "we listen to the world scream."

Outside, a jet passed overhead, contrail slicing the sky at a carefully approved speed.

Kade watched it go.

"Mach .92," he said softly.

Zara nodded.

"The line everyone's been told not to cross."

They stood there in the hangar, the first crude model frozen on the screen between them—not an answer, not a weapon, not even a breakthrough yet.

Just a mirror.

And for the first time, Kade understood exactly why someone, somewhere, had decided fifty years ago that civilian airplanes should never be allowed to go this fast over land.

Because once you could *see* what was buried…

You could never unsee it.

Chapter 11

Chuck Yeager's LOGBOOK

October 14, 1947

It started as a footnote.

Not a headline. Not a scandal. Not even a mystery—at least not the kind people wrote books about. Just a thin thread Zara pulled out of a haystack of old government archives and forgotten technical appendices, the kind of places history went to die when it wasn't useful anymore.

She didn't find it by searching for *Chuck Yeager*.

She found it by searching for a phrase Kade had used without thinking:

locks in

That was how it always happened. The most important clues didn't arrive wearing their real names. They arrived wearing ordinary words.

Zara sat at Kade's workbench at two in the morning, the hangar dark except for the blue-white glow of her screens. The Lear loomed behind her—white, stripped, quiet—its shadow stretching across the floor like something listening.

Kade stood with his back to the fuselage, arms folded, coffee cooling in his hand. He wasn't tired. Not really. He was in that strange space where your body wanted rest but your mind refused it.

Zara clicked through folders labeled in dull, bureaucratic language:

AERODYNAMIC EFFECTS — TRANSONIC REGIME
STRUCTURAL RESPONSE — FLIGHT TEST ANOMALIES
PRESSURE SIGNATURES — OVERLAND OPERATIONS
NOISE COMPLAINTS — PUBLIC IMPACT

The last one made her smirk.

"Of course," she muttered.

Kade didn't respond. He'd learned that when Zara went quiet like this, she was hunting. Not browsing. Hunting.

Minutes passed.

Then she stopped.

Not dramatically—just a pause, a stillness in her shoulders, like someone had stepped into the room behind her.

Kade felt it.

"What?" he asked.

Zara didn't look up.

"I found something that doesn't want to be found," she said.

"That's your specialty."

She exhaled through her nose, almost amused.

"This one's older."

She rotated the screen toward him.

It wasn't a memo. Not exactly.

It was a scan of a small, worn, spiral-bound notebook page. The kind a pilot would keep in a flight bag. Paper yellowed. Edges softened. The handwriting clean and tight—military disciplined, not casual.

At the top, in block letters:

FLT NOTE — TRANS REGIME / STRUCT RESP CHUCK YEAGER

Kade stared.

He didn't feel awe.

He felt recognition.

Not of Yeager himself, but of the handwriting's intent— this was a man writing something down because he didn't trust anyone else to notice it.

Zara zoomed in.

The entry was short. The kind of short that meant the writer had more to say but knew better than to say it on paper.

Kade read.

Speed: M .90–.93
Alt: high / stable
Condition: "locks"
Airframe response shifts — coherent
Not buffet
Not flutter
Terrain correlation suspected
Water crossing changes response
Hard ground = stable harmonic
Soft ground = scatter
Repeatable
Engineers dismiss as structural resonance
Recommend: measure, don't filter

Kade felt his jaw tighten.

It was his flight.

Sixty years earlier.

He looked at Zara.

"Is that real?" he asked quietly.

Zara didn't blink.

"It's buried under three layers of 'structural response' documentation and one layer of scanned microfilm that someone mislabeled on purpose," she said. "So yes. It's real."

Kade stared at the screen again.

The word that hit hardest wasn't *terrain*.

It was *filter*.

Recommend: measure, don't filter.

Kade swallowed.

"Why would anyone filter it?" he asked.

Zara clicked again.

Another page appeared—typed this time. A formal memo. Sparse. Cold. No emotion. Redactions like black teeth.

NACA / USAF FLIGHT TEST REVIEW
SUBJECT: PRESSURE SIGNATURE ARTIFACTS — TRANSONIC OVERLAND

Most of it was redacted.

But the unredacted portions were worse because they didn't explain anything. They simply *moved something out of view*.

Recommendation: discontinue overland transonic runs pending further evaluation of "pressure signature artifacts."
Public framing: noise complaints / community impact.
Internal framing: defer.
Data handling: restrict distribution.
Note: "terrain-coupled effects" not to be referenced in general circulation documentation.

Kade felt a cold, slow heaviness settle in his chest.

He wasn't angry yet.

Anger required certainty.

This was still that earlier stage—where your brain tried to protect you by offering alternatives.

Coincidence. Misinterpretation. Old jargon.

But the alignment was too clean.

Mach .90–.93.
Locks.
Water changes response.
Hard ground stabilizes.
Soft ground scatters.

That wasn't poetic language.

That was a pilot trying to describe something physics didn't have a polite label for yet.

Zara leaned back in her chair.

"That's the first time I've seen the word 'terrain' in a transonic structural note," she said. "It shouldn't be there. It doesn't belong in that category."

Kade stared at the black redaction bars.

"So they found it," he said.

Zara nodded.

"And they buried it," she replied.

Kade walked a slow circle, boots scuffing lightly against concrete. He stopped beside the Lear, resting a hand on the cool metal as if grounding himself.

"Why?" he asked.

Zara didn't answer immediately.

Because this was the kind of question that made people invent wars.

She tapped, bringing up another document. Not a memo this time—a clipped newspaper scan. Grainy. Local. A small-town complaint story about sonic booms rattling windows. A quote from a homemaker. A line about children crying. A mention of livestock spooking.

Then a government statement beneath it: *Public safety concerns. Noise mitigation. Flights curtailed.*

Zara zoomed in on the date.

Kade read it.

He felt his stomach drop.

The sonic boom complaints were real.

But they weren't the first domino.

They were the mask placed over a different one.

Zara pulled up a final item. A routing slip. Nothing dramatic. A bureaucratic artifact that looked like it belonged in a trash bin.

Except it carried names.

Not the names you wanted.

The names you didn't.

A chain of internal distribution. A "do not circulate" stamp. A signature line from someone in the executive branch that should not have been attached to flight-test minutiae.

Kade stared at it, then at Zara.

She didn't say the name out loud.

She didn't have to.

Kade exhaled slowly.

"Okay," he said. "So the public got noise, and the inside people got silence."

Zara nodded.

"And Yaeger got dismissed," she said.

Kade looked back at Yeager's handwritten note.

Engineers dismiss as structural resonance.

Recommend: measure, don't filter.

Kade pictured it in his head: a test pilot noticing something real, trying to convince men in white shirts and ties that the airplane was telling them the earth was answering, and being met with polite smiles and technical language that said *thank you for your service, now shut up.*

It wasn't hard to imagine. Kade had lived versions of it his entire life.

The difference was scale.

This wasn't a bad manager.

This wasn't a corrupt client.

This was... the system.

Zara's voice pulled him back.

"Look at the dates," she said.

Kade leaned in.

She had arranged the files in a timeline—Yeager's notes, the internal memo, the public noise framing, the flight curtailment.

Then she slid another timeline beneath it.

Supersonic policy discussions. Early FAA formation. Overland restrictions evolving into formal bans.

The two timelines touched like gears.

Not perfectly. Not cleanly.

But enough.

"What you're looking at," Zara said quietly, "is not a ban created by physics."

Kade felt the hangar air turn colder.

"It's a ban created by control," he said.

Zara nodded.

"And control always needs a public reason," she said. "Noise is perfect. Everyone understands noise. Everyone hates noise. Noise can be measured. Noise can be litigated."

She let that sit, then added:

"But noise isn't the threat."

Kade stared at the Lear.

At his stripped-out cabin.

At the exposed ribs that carried vibration like a confession.

"What is?" he asked.

Zara looked at him the way she did when she was about to say something that would permanently change the shape of a room.

"Seeing," she said.

Kade didn't speak.

Zara slid her tablet toward him again, zooming into Yeager's handwriting.

Terrain correlation suspected.

Kade read it slowly.

Then he looked up.

"They didn't know what it was," he said.

Zara's smile was thin.

"They knew enough to be afraid of it," she replied.

Kade took a breath, then another.

He felt, unexpectedly, a strange kind of respect for the past—because those men had seen the edge of something they didn't understand and chosen to keep it from everyone else until they could.

That was human.

It was also unforgivable.

"Why didn't it become useful then?" Kade asked.

Zara shrugged.

"Computing," she said. "Sensors. Modeling. Inversion algorithms. Data storage. AI. Everything you need to turn signals into images."

She tapped the screen where Yeager's note lived.

"Yeager could feel it," she said. "But he couldn't *prove* it."

Kade's mouth went dry.

"And now?" he asked.

Zara's gaze held his.

"Now you can," she said.

The hangar went quiet again—quiet in a different way than before. Like even the building was listening.

Kade looked at Yeager's handwritten note one more time.

He imagined the pilot at altitude, feeling the airplane lock into coherence, realizing the sensation wasn't inside the jet at all—realizing the ground was speaking back—and writing it down because he didn't know what else to do with it.

Kade knew that feeling.

He'd felt it at Mach .92.

The difference was this: Yeager had nowhere to take it.

Kade did.

He looked at Zara.

"What else did you find?" he asked.

Zara hesitated.

Not because she didn't know.

Because she did.

"There's a second set of files," she said. "Not in the aviation archives."

Kade's eyes narrowed.

"Where?"

Zara glanced toward the hangar doors as if the answer might be standing outside.

"Energy," she said. "Natural resources. Subsurface. Seismic."

Kade felt his throat tighten.

Oil.

Of course.

Zara continued, voice controlled.

"The language changes," she said. "They don't talk about sonic booms. They talk about 'unintended interrogation.' They talk about 'signature leakage.' They talk about 'mapping risk.'"

Kade let out a slow breath.

"And they never say Mach .92?"

Zara smiled faintly.

"They don't need to," she said. "They describe the condition without naming it. Like they're afraid the name itself is a key."

Kade stared at the Lear again.

A jet he'd bought like a toy.

A machine that had just reached back into the 1950s, touched a buried secret, and brought it forward into a world that could finally understand it.

He didn't feel triumphant.

He felt responsible.

That was worse.

Zara closed the files and shut the tablet screen, the glow disappearing instantly, leaving the hangar darker than before.

"What do we do with this?" Kade asked.

Zara didn't hesitate this time.

"We treat it like it's real," she said. "Because it is."

Kade nodded slowly.

"And we don't fly faster," Zara added.

The words landed differently now.

Not as caution.

As warning.

Kade's eyes lifted.

"Someone told Yeager that," he said.

Zara's expression didn't change.

"They didn't have to," she said. "They just took away the runway."

Kade stood there for a long moment, listening to the quiet, feeling the weight of all those years compressed into the space between two sentences.

Then he said the only thing that mattered.

"Okay," he said. "Then we build our own runway."

Zara's smile returned—small, sharp, delighted.

"That," she said, "is why it's you."

Kade looked at the Lear one more time.

White. Old. Innocent-looking.

And suddenly he understood exactly why the sound barrier had become a public myth and a private boundary.

Not because breaking it was dangerous.

Because what it revealed was.

Chapter 12

DON'T FLY FASTER

The first sign wasn't dramatic.

There was no knock on the hangar door. No black SUVs idling outside. No voice lowering itself into menace on the other end of a phone call.

It was an email.

Subject line: **Routine Airspace Inquiry**

That was how these things always started—small enough to ignore if you didn't know better, ordinary enough to pass for coincidence if you wanted to stay comfortable.

Kade didn't.

He stood in the hangar with the Lear behind him and Frank's old Ford parked just outside, phone in his hand, reading the message for the third time.

Mr. Vance,
We are conducting a routine review of recent high-subsonic operations in controlled airspace.
Your Learjet 25B registration has appeared in proximity

to several monitoring thresholds.
No action is required at this time.
We simply request clarification regarding operational profiles and intended use.

—FAA Airspace Compliance

Kade smiled faintly.

"Routine," he said out loud.

Zara leaned back in her chair, arms crossed, eyes never leaving the screen she'd pulled the email onto.

"They don't ask unless they already know," she said.

Kade nodded. "And they don't say 'thresholds' unless someone tripped one."

"Or brushed one," Zara corrected. "Hard enough to get noticed. Soft enough to stay deniable."

The hangar felt different today. Less like a workshop, more like a quiet room after bad news—no raised voices, no panic, just a subtle tightening of everything that mattered.

Maggie lay near the door, head on her paws, watching both of them with mild suspicion. She didn't understand emails, but she understood tone.

Kade walked to the Lear and rested a hand on the fuselage, feeling the cool metal under his palm.

"They didn't say Mach," he said.

Zara shook her head. "They won't. That's the point."

She swiped to another screen, pulling up a timeline she'd been building since Yeager's logbook.

"Watch this," she said.

She highlighted a band across the graph—airspace monitoring systems, acoustic arrays, pressure sensors scattered across the country, most of them publicly described as *environmental* or *infrastructure health* tools.

"None of these are officially designed to detect speed violations," she continued. "They're designed to detect *anomalies*."

Kade glanced at her.

"And Mach .92 creates one."

Zara nodded. "Not a boom. Not a violation. A *pattern*."

She zoomed in further.

"At certain speeds, pressure waves don't just trail the aircraft. They interfere. Stack. Reinforce. The result isn't noise—it's coherence."

Kade felt the echo of the hum in his spine just thinking about it.

"And coherence," Zara said, "is impossible to ignore if you're looking for it."

Kade turned back to the email.

"They're asking what I intend to do," he said.

"They're giving you a chance to lie," Zara replied calmly.

Kade didn't answer right away.

He walked outside, leaned against the Ford's front fender, and stared out at the runway beyond the fence. Planes came and went in the distance—regional jets, business traffic, all of them moving briskly but obediently, never quite touching the line everyone pretended was about noise.

Frank's truck ticked quietly as it cooled, metal contracting the way it always had.

Kade thought about Yeager.

About a man who'd felt something real, written it down, and watched the runway disappear under his feet without anyone ever saying *why*.

He came back inside.

"They didn't tell him to stop," Kade said. "They just made it impossible to continue."

Zara nodded. "That's the cleanest way."

"So this is the modern version."

"Yes," she said. "Mission Possible."

Kade smiled despite himself.

"You make it sound friendly."

"It is," Zara replied. "Friendly pressure is the most effective kind. No villains. No resistance to rally against. Just boundaries."

Kade set the phone down on the workbench.

"What happens if I reply?" he asked.

Zara didn't hesitate.

"You'll be placed into a box," she said. "Flight profiles defined. Speed envelopes informally suggested. Insurance questions. Maintenance audits. The kind of friction that makes people slow down without realizing they're being slowed."

"And if I don't reply?"

"Then the box gets built anyway," Zara said. "Just smaller."

Kade ran a hand through his hair.

"So either way…"

"They don't want you flying faster," she finished.

Silence stretched again.

Kade glanced at the Lear's cockpit, the analog gauges staring back like they always did—truthful, unfiltered, indifferent to policy.

"They still think this is about speed," he said.

Zara's smile was thin. "They always do. Speed is easy to regulate. *What speed reveals* is harder."

She stepped closer to the Lear, lowering her voice instinctively.

"This isn't about preventing a sonic boom," she continued. "It's about preventing a picture."

Kade felt the weight of that settle in.

"You said this would get classified retroactively," he said.

Zara nodded. "That email is the first draft."

Kade laughed once, quietly. Not from humor—from recognition.

"Yeager didn't have AI," he said. "Didn't have sensors. Didn't have compute."

Zara met his eyes.

"But you do."

The hangar hummed softly—servers, cooling fans, the faint electrical presence of systems coming online whether permission had been granted or not.

Kade walked to the whiteboard and erased a single word at the top.

HYPOTHESIS

He wrote a new one beneath it.

MODEL

Zara watched him do it, a slow grin spreading.

"They don't want you flying faster," she said again.

Kade capped the marker.

"Good," he replied. "Because I don't need to."

Zara's eyes sharpened.

"You're thinking lateral," she said.

"I'm thinking *orthogonal*," Kade corrected. "Speed is just one axis."

Zara nodded, already seeing it.

"Altitude. Mass. Configuration. Repetition."

"And routes," Kade added. "Places no one watches closely because nothing ever happens there."

She smiled. "Until now."

Kade picked up his phone again, reread the email once more, then typed a brief response.

Thank you for reaching out.
Operations are currently limited to maintenance verification and pilot familiarization.
No deviations planned.
Happy to coordinate if needed.

He hit send.

Zara watched without comment.

"That buys us time," she said.

"Not much."

"No," she agreed. "But enough."

Kade looked at the Lear again—not as a jet, not as a weapon, not even as a discovery.

As a tool.

"They think the boundary is speed," he said.

Zara nodded. "Because that's where it was last time."

Kade smiled slowly.

"Well," he said, "history has a habit of repeating itself… until someone changes the variables."

Zara closed her laptop and picked up her jacket.

"Then we build quietly," she said. "We verify without broadcasting. We map places where the answer is already known."

Kade nodded.

"And when they finally realize what this is?"

Zara paused at the hangar door.

"Then it won't matter whether they tell you not to fly faster," she said. "Because the mirror will already be built."

Outside, a jet crossed the sky, contrail clean and white, safely below the line everyone agreed not to cross.

Kade watched it go.

Mach .92 wasn't a rebellion.

It was a reminder.

And reminders had a way of coming back—no matter how many runways you closed.

Chapter 13

INSTRUMENTING THE LEAR

They didn't order anything exotic.

That was the first rule.

No custom enclosures. No defense contractors. No specialty vendors whose invoices triggered follow-up questions six months later. Everything arrived in plain cardboard boxes with boring labels and return addresses that blended into the noise of modern logistics.

Accelerometers.
Strain gauges.
Pressure transducers.
Timing modules.
Cabling rated for environments nobody ever asked about.

Off-the-shelf truth.

Zara spread it all out on folding tables in the hangar, arranging components with the calm precision of someone assembling a bomb—or defusing one. Hard to tell which, sometimes.

Kade watched, hands in his pockets, coffee untouched.

"This is the part where you tell me it's not complicated," he said.

Zara didn't look up. "It's not complicated."

He waited.

"It's just unforgiving," she added.

That sounded more accurate.

They worked with the Lear powered down, doors open, sunlight washing through the stripped cabin and glinting off exposed ribs and wiring runs. The airplane looked halfway between a museum exhibit and a patient on an operating table.

"This jet already tells the truth," Zara said, running a hand along the structure. "We're just teaching it how to remember."

She started with the seat rails—Kade's seat first. Not because it was convenient, but because that was where the phenomenon had introduced itself.

"Your body noticed before your instruments," she said. "That matters."

They mounted sensors where vibration converged, not where it was loudest. Zara explained as she worked, not lecturing—just narrating decisions like a chess player talking through a position.

"Most engineers chase amplitude," she said. "Big signals. Big movements. That's not what this is."

She paused, repositioned a sensor a few inches.

"This is coherence," she continued. "The interesting part isn't how strong it is. It's how *organized*."

Kade nodded. He understood that instinctively. The Lear hadn't shaken him. It had aligned with him.

They ran wiring along existing channels, careful not to introduce new resonance paths. No shortcuts. No zip ties where clamps belonged.

"Anything that lies to us gets removed," Zara said.

By mid-afternoon, the Lear's cabin looked like a skeleton wired for thought. Not pretty. Not hidden. Functional in a way that felt almost surgical.

They didn't power anything yet.

Instead, Zara pulled out a laptop and opened a block of code so bare it looked unfinished.

"This is the listener," she said.

"That's it?"

"That's it," she replied. "No filtering. No smoothing. No assumptions."

Kade frowned. "That's going to be noisy."

"Yes," Zara said. "And that's the point."

She glanced at him.

"Filtering is how Yeager lost it," she said quietly. "They decided what *shouldn't* matter before they knew what *did*."

Kade felt the weight of that settle.

They finished mounting the last sensor just before sunset. The hangar was quiet except for the faint clink of tools and Maggie's slow breathing near the door.

Zara stepped back, wiped her hands on a rag, and nodded once.

"Okay," she said. "Now we fly."

Kade raised an eyebrow. "High and fast?"

She shook her head.

"No," she said. "Low. Slow. Boring."

He smiled.

"Good," he said. "I've got just the airplane."

They took the 210 the next morning.

Frank's old bird sat exactly where it always had, paint sun-faded, lines familiar enough that Kade could've preflighted it blindfolded. No one gave it a second look as they taxied out. No monitoring thresholds. No interest.

That was the beauty of it.

They climbed to a few thousand feet and leveled off over land Kade knew by heart. Oil country. Places where the geology was already written down in public filings and forgotten reports.

Zara watched her screen as the sensors began to populate—nothing dramatic at first. Just noise. Messy, overlapping, unremarkable.

Then she adjusted a parameter.

Not a filter.

A *time alignment*.

The data shifted.

"Hold that heading," she said.

Kade held it.

The noise thinned.

Not vanished. Organized.

Zara's breathing changed.

"Again," she said. "Turn ten degrees right."

Kade did.

The pattern changed instantly.

She looked up at him, eyes wide now.

"It's there," she said. "Even down here."

Kade kept his voice calm. "Different?"

"Yes," she said. "Lower resolution. Shorter penetration. But the same *logic*."

She zoomed in, cross-referencing against known survey data.

Then she stopped moving altogether.

Kade glanced over. "What?"

Zara swallowed.

"It matches," she said.

Silence filled the cockpit.

"Matches what?" Kade asked.

She turned the screen toward him.

A crude subsurface profile—nothing pretty, nothing polished—just enough structure to be unmistakable.

"That's a known formation," she said. "Public data. We didn't teach it that."

Kade felt something in his chest loosen and tighten at the same time.

"So the Lear—"

"—is the high-altitude instrument," Zara finished. "The 210 is the confirmation tool."

She looked back at the screen.

"And the world," she said softly, "has been screaming this whole time."

They flew on for another hour, quiet, deliberate, collecting without chasing. When they landed, neither of them spoke until the engine shut down and the prop ticked to a stop.

Back in the hangar, Zara closed the laptop and sat heavily on a crate.

"This isn't a fluke," she said. "It's a system."

Kade leaned against the 210, hand resting on the same skin Frank's had touched decades earlier.

"They were watching the wrong thing," he said.

Zara nodded. "Speed. Noise. Altitude."

"And ignoring the obvious," Kade added.

She smiled faintly. "That the ground doesn't care who's listening."

They stood there together—old airplane, new jet, quiet hangar—surrounded by machines that didn't lie and a discovery that no longer belonged to one man, one era, or one excuse.

Kade finally broke the silence.

"They told Yeager not to fly faster," he said.

Zara looked at him.

"And you didn't," she said.

Kade smiled.

"No," he replied. "I flew smarter."

The Lear sat behind them, white and unassuming, wired now with ears sharp enough to hear secrets buried half a century ago.

And somewhere beyond the fence, systems watched the skies—still focused on speed, still blind below the noise floor.

For now.

Chapter 14

KNOWN GROUND

They didn't call it a test flight.

That would've implied uncertainty.

They called it a **confirmation run**.

Kade chose the location the way he chose runways—places with history, places that had already been measured, drilled, argued over, and forgotten. Ground that had been sliced open by engineers long before anyone worried about who might be listening from above.

Oil country.

Not the romantic kind. No pump jacks nodding politely for tourists. This was older land—dry, layered, scarred by decades of seismic surveys and core samples. The geology here was public record, buried under regulatory filings and PDFs nobody opened unless they had a reason.

Which made it perfect.

If the model was wrong, it would fail quietly.

If it was right…

Kade preflighted the Lear himself, moving slowly, deliberately. No audience. No rush. The jet looked unchanged—white paint, clean lines, nothing about it advertising what had been bolted into its bones.

Zara stood off to the side, tablet in hand, not watching him so much as watching *the air*—conditions, pressure, stability. She was thinking three steps ahead, as always.

"Same profile," she said. "Same speed. Same altitude."

Kade nodded. "No heroics."

"None," she agreed. "We don't need them."

They took off just after noon, climbing into a sky that felt indifferent—high, wide, empty. The kind of sky pilots loved because it didn't argue.

At altitude, the Lear settled in quickly, almost eagerly, like it recognized the routine now.

Mach .92 arrived without drama.

No push. No chase.

Just alignment.

The hum returned immediately, locking into place with the same calm authority as before. Zara didn't comment. She didn't need to.

Her screen was already alive.

Raw data flowed first—chaotic, layered, ugly. Then, slowly, inexorably, it began to organize.

"Hold," she said.

Kade held.

The Lear flew like it was on rails.

Below them, the land unfolded in muted tones—ancient formations, subtle folds, nothing dramatic to the untrained eye. But Zara's display began to change.

Contours emerged.

Not images—not yet—but **relationships**. Density gradients. Boundaries. Discontinuities.

She swallowed.

"Okay," she said quietly. "There it is."

Kade kept his eyes forward. "Talk to me."

"This formation," she said, highlighting a region on the screen, "should be here."

Another shape resolved.

"And this one," she continued, voice steady now, "shouldn't."

Kade's grip tightened slightly on the yoke.

"What do you mean shouldn't?"

She pulled up a second dataset—public seismic records from the same region. Old surveys. Approved. Sanitized.

The comparison was brutal.

"There's a void," she said. "A structure. Too regular to be natural."

"How big?" Kade asked.

Zara hesitated.

"Big enough to matter."

The hum in the Lear deepened, steady and unwavering, like the airplane itself was insisting on being heard.

Zara's fingers flew now, refining, cross-checking, overlaying. The crude model sharpened—not into a picture, but into something worse.

A **confirmation**.

"This area was surveyed three times," she said. "All three reports show… nothing."

She looked up at Kade.

"And yet," she said, "here it is."

Kade exhaled slowly.

"Could it be error?"

She shook her head. "Error doesn't repeat like this. Error doesn't have edges."

The Lear crossed another invisible boundary in the sky, and the signal tightened again, crisp and undeniable.

Zara stared at the screen.

"This isn't oil," she said.

Kade didn't ask how she knew.

"This is infrastructure," she continued. "Subsurface. Engineered. And deliberately absent from public records."

The word *deliberately* landed heavy.

Kade glanced at the horizon, then back at the instruments. Everything was green. Calm. Ordinary.

Above ground, the world was exactly as advertised.

Below it...

"This isn't just about mapping," he said.

Zara nodded. "No. This is about **exposure**."

She leaned back in her chair, hands trembling just slightly now.

"Do you know what it costs to hide something like this?" she asked.

Kade didn't answer.

"Because I do," she said. "Financially. Politically. Logistically. You don't do this unless the alternative is worse."

The Lear hummed on, indifferent to human motives.

Zara saved the file, naming it carefully.

KNOWN_GROUND_01

She didn't add *test*.
She didn't add *draft*.

They flew the rest of the route in silence, neither of them needing to say what was already clear.

On descent, the hum unwound slowly, reluctantly, like it didn't want to let go of the conversation.

Back in the hangar, engines cooling, Kade sat longer than usual, hands resting on his thighs, feeling the afterimage of vibration in his bones.

Zara stood behind him, screen dark now, her reflection faint in the cockpit glass.

"This changes everything," she said.

Kade nodded. "That's usually when people get nervous."

She smiled thinly. "That's usually when they make mistakes."

Kade climbed out and stood on the hangar floor, looking at the Lear like it had just crossed a line no one had drawn on a map.

"They buried this once," he said.

Zara joined him.

"Yes," she replied. "And they'll try again."

Kade looked at Frank's old Ford outside, the 210 parked beside it, both machines survivors of eras that hadn't known what to fear yet.

"They can't unsee this," he said.

Zara met his gaze.

"Neither can we."

The hangar fell quiet again—not the comfortable quiet of work well done, but the charged silence that came just before consequences.

Kade broke it.

"Next," he said, "we find out who owns what we just uncovered."

Zara nodded.

"And who's willing to kill to keep it buried," she added.

Kade didn't argue.

The Lear sat behind them, white and unremarkable, its ears now tuned to a world that had been lying quietly beneath everyone's feet.

And for the first time, the question wasn't whether the discovery was real.

It was whether the world was ready to see it.

Chapter 15

THE ANOMALY

It didn't announce itself.

That was the problem.

The anomaly appeared the way real problems always did —not as a spike, not as an alarm, but as something that *fit too well*. Something that made a model behave better than it should have.

Zara noticed it first, not because she was looking for trouble, but because she wasn't.

She sat at the folding table in the hangar late that night, laptop balanced on a stack of old sectional charts, the Lear looming behind her like a white question mark. Kade was across the hangar, cleaning tools that didn't need cleaning, Maggie asleep at his feet.

Normal.

That was the danger.

Zara was running a validation pass against public subsurface datasets—nothing sensitive, nothing classified. Old seismic surveys. Oil-field maps that had been scanned, redacted, rescanned, and uploaded so many times no one remembered who owned them anymore.

The goal was simple:

Prove the model wrong.

That was always the first real test.

She fed in the Lear data from the confirmation run—not the raw vibration traces, just the abstracted interaction curves. The kind of thing any analyst would dismiss as noise if they weren't paying attention.

The model refreshed.

Zara frowned.

She ran it again.

Same result.

The predicted subsurface boundaries aligned more cleanly than they should have. Fault lines sharpened. Density gradients tightened. The model's confidence intervals shrank.

Not by much.

But enough.

"That's not possible," she murmured.

She leaned closer to the screen, eyes narrowing. Public seismic data was messy by nature—averaged, smoothed, politically neutered. It was never this crisp.

Unless…

She pulled up the same dataset without Kade's flight overlay.

The model degraded immediately.

Blurry. Uncertain. Honest.

Zara felt a chill creep up her spine.

She toggled the Lear data back on.

Clarity returned.

Not perfect. Not miraculous.

Just… *better*.

The worst kind of better.

She didn't smile.

She didn't celebrate.

She checked the access logs.

That was when her stomach tightened.

There was a new query in the system.

Not from her.
Not from Kade.

Someone else had accessed the same regional seismic data less than an hour earlier.

She clicked deeper.

The request wasn't broad. It wasn't exploratory.

It was surgical.

Historical overlays.
Comparative depth models.
Correlation against legacy surveys.

The kind of queries only someone deeply familiar with the basin would think to run.

Zara sat back slowly.

"Kade," she said.

He looked up immediately. "What is it?"

"Someone else just asked the same question we did."

He crossed the hangar in three strides.

"Who?"

She shook her head. "Not 'who.' *What*."

She turned the screen toward him.

"This is a licensed industry portal," she said. "Paid access. Corporate credentials. Perfectly legitimate."

Kade scanned the log.

"So they weren't watching us," he said.

"No," Zara replied. "They were watching *their data*."

She pulled up a side-by-side comparison—before and after.

"The model improved," she said quietly. "Enough that someone noticed."

Kade exhaled slowly.

"So the ground answered," he said. "And the people who listen to the ground heard it."

Zara nodded.

"This is how it spreads," she said. "Not through flight tracking. Not through surveillance. Through professionals realizing something changed without them touching it."

She zoomed in on the timestamp.

"Whatever we did," she continued, "propagated into existing systems. Just enough to wake someone up."

Kade leaned against the table, eyes on the screen.

"How long?" he asked.

Zara hesitated.

"Minutes to hours," she said. "Not instant. But fast."

"Fast enough."

"Yes."

Silence settled between them, heavier now.

"This is why they buried it," Kade said.

Zara nodded. "Because once it's useful, it can't be contained."

She closed the dataset and leaned back, rubbing her temples.

"This isn't detection," she said. "It's *recognition*."

Kade stared at the Lear.

"So they didn't see us fly," he said. "They saw the earth answer differently."

Zara met his gaze.

"And that's worse."

Kade's phone buzzed on the workbench.

He didn't look at it yet.

Zara glanced at it, then back at him.

"That'll be oil," she said. "Or someone who works for them."

Kade didn't move.

"How sure are you?" he asked.

Zara didn't hesitate.

"Because seismic people don't call the FAA," she said. "They call money."

The phone buzzed again.

Unknown number. Texas area code.

Kade picked it up this time, eyes never leaving Zara.

"Yeah," he said.

Zara watched his face change as the voice on the other end spoke—slowly, professionally, already acting as if the conversation was overdue.

She didn't need to hear the words.

She already knew what had happened.

Somewhere far away, a geophysicist had leaned back in a chair and said:

That's not supposed to be there.

And from that moment on, the clock had started.

Kade listened for a few seconds longer, then raised a hand toward Zara—not a stop, just a *wait*.

He ended the call without speaking.

He set the phone down carefully.

"They noticed," he said.

Zara nodded. "Of course they did."

Kade looked back at the Lear—white, stripped, quiet.

"No one watched us fly," he said.

"No," Zara replied. "They watched the ground get smarter."

Maggie lifted her head, sensing the shift, tail thumping once against the concrete.

Kade took a breath, then another.

"Okay," he said. "Now it makes sense."

Zara met his eyes.

"Welcome to oil country," she said.

Chapter 16

OIL COUNTRY

Money noticed before government ever did.

That was the rule.

Regulators reacted to violations. Intelligence agencies reacted to threats. But money—real money—reacted to *possibility*. It didn't wait for permission. It didn't need certainty. It just needed the scent of something that could change the board.

Kade felt it before the call came.

Not paranoia. Not intuition in the mystical sense. Just pattern recognition—the same subtle tightening he'd felt in the Lear at Mach .92, when the hum organized itself into something deliberate.

He was back in the hangar, late afternoon light slanting across the concrete, when Zara froze mid-sentence.

She was standing at the folding table, laptop open, eyes locked on something she hadn't meant to find yet.

"Kade," she said.

He looked up. "What?"

"Someone just queried seismic data from our confirmation run."

The air shifted.

"That's not public yet," he said.

"No," Zara agreed. "It shouldn't be queryable at all."

She turned the screen toward him.

A backend access log. Clean. Professional. No sloppiness. Whoever had pulled the data hadn't brute-forced anything or tripped alarms. They'd come in through legitimate pathways—paid subscriptions, licensed portals, industry credentials.

Oil.

"They didn't ask for the raw," Zara continued. "They asked for *historical overlays*."

Kade exhaled slowly.

"So they're checking us against what they already know."

"Or what they *suspect*," she said.

Maggie lifted her head, ears pricking, as if she sensed the shift in tone.

Kade leaned against the Lear's fuselage, arms folded.

"How long?" he asked.

"Minutes," Zara replied. "They moved fast."

That told him everything.

This wasn't curiosity.
It was confirmation.

The phone rang five minutes later.

Unknown number. Texas area code.

Kade stared at it for a moment longer than necessary, then answered.

"Vance," he said.

The voice on the other end was calm, polished, friendly in the way only people with leverage could afford to be.

"Mr. Vance," the man said. "My name is Caleb Rhodes. I represent a private energy consortium with assets in the Permian and beyond."

Kade didn't respond.

"We've been made aware," Rhodes continued smoothly, "that you're operating a unique aerial survey platform. Experimental, perhaps. Early stage."

Zara mouthed *wow*.

Kade kept his voice neutral. "You've got the wrong number."

Rhodes chuckled lightly. "If that were true, you wouldn't still be on the line."

Kade glanced at Zara. She was already pulling threads, mapping corporate structures faster than Rhodes could pretend not to be obvious.

"What do you want?" Kade asked.

"Conversation," Rhodes replied. "Discretion. And potentially, partnership."

Kade closed his eyes for half a second.

"Funny," he said. "The FAA just wanted clarification."

"Yes," Rhodes said without missing a beat. "That was... predictable."

The implication hung there, unspoken but unmistakable.

"We believe," Rhodes continued, "that what you've developed has applications far beyond traditional seismic methods. Faster. Cleaner. Less... intrusive."

Zara snorted softly.

Rhodes pressed on.

"Imagine mapping subsurface structures without trucks. Without explosives. Without permits that take years and invite scrutiny."

Kade's jaw tightened.

"You mean without anyone knowing you were looking," he said.

There was a pause this time.

Then Rhodes said, "I prefer to think of it as efficiency."

Kade looked back at the Lear—white, quiet, pretending to be nothing more than an old jet.

"And what makes you think I'd sell that?" he asked.

"I don't," Rhodes said calmly. "Not outright."

Zara's fingers flew across her keyboard. She leaned in close, whispering.

"Caleb Rhodes. Former VP, Lone Star Energy. Now sits on three private boards. Heavy political donations. No government role, but deep ties."

Rhodes continued, unaware or unconcerned.

"I think you're a realist," he said. "And realists understand leverage. The kind you've stumbled into tends to attract attention—from parties far less polite than my clients."

Kade smiled faintly.

"That sounds like a threat."

"Not at all," Rhodes replied. "It's an offer to get ahead of one."

Kade felt the shape of the trap now.

Oil didn't want to stop him.
It wanted to own him.

"Let me guess," Kade said. "You want exclusive access."

"Limited," Rhodes said quickly. "Discreet. Controlled. We'd fund further development. Provide legal cover. Keep this... manageable."

Zara shook her head slowly.

"And if I say no?" Kade asked.

Rhodes didn't hesitate.

"Then others will call," he said. "Less patient ones. And eventually, someone will decide you're not worth the uncertainty."

The line went quiet.

Not dead.
Just waiting.

Kade leaned against the workbench, eyes never leaving the Lear.

"You're moving fast," he said. "That usually means you're afraid of something."

Rhodes laughed softly. "We're afraid of being late."

That was the truth.

Kade felt it settle—this wasn't about oil. Not really. Oil was just the first domino. The first industry big enough, rich enough, desperate enough to recognize what had just become possible.

"Here's what's going to happen," Kade said evenly. "I'm not selling. I'm not partnering. And I'm not flying for you."

Rhodes sighed. "That's unfortunate."

"But," Kade continued, "you're going to hang up and tell your clients one thing."

"Oh?"

"That whatever you think you saw," Kade said, "you didn't see all of it."

Silence stretched again.

"That's a bold position," Rhodes said finally.

Kade smiled.

"So is calling me this early."

He ended the call.

Zara looked at him, eyes bright, pulse visible at her throat.

"Well," she said. "That escalated."

Kade nodded. "Oil always does."

She closed her laptop, exhaled slowly.

"That was your first offer," she said. "Which means…"

"It won't be the last," Kade finished.

He walked to the hangar door and looked out at the runway, the sky beyond it wide and deceptively calm.

"They don't want this exposed," Zara said quietly. "They want it monetized."

Kade nodded. "Same instinct. Different language."

Zara met his gaze.

"And if oil knows," she said, "government won't be far behind."

Kade's expression didn't change.

"They already are," he said.

He looked back at the Lear, then at the 210, then at Frank's old truck—three machines from three eras, all built before anyone imagined the world would become this complicated.

"This just stopped being a science problem," Zara said.

Kade nodded once.

"And started being a control problem," he replied.

Outside, the sun dipped lower, casting long shadows across the tarmac.

Somewhere far away, money was moving—quietly, urgently—trying to get in front of a discovery that didn't care who owned it.

And Kade understood something with perfect clarity.

The most dangerous moment wasn't when someone threatened you.

It was when they offered to buy you.

Chapter 17

THE SECOND CALL

The second call didn't come from Texas.

It didn't come with a name, either.

It came as a favor.

Kade was alone in the hangar when it happened—Zara had stepped out to take a call of her own, Maggie stretched out in a patch of sunlight near the door. The Lear sat silent, white skin glowing softly, pretending it was just another retired jet waiting for a paint job.

Kade was elbow-deep in a wiring bay, tracing a run that didn't quite sit right, when his phone vibrated in his pocket.

No ring.

Just a single pulse.

He straightened slowly, wiped his hands on a rag, and looked at the screen.

No Caller ID.

He didn't answer immediately.

He never did with numbers like that.

The phone vibrated again—once, patient, almost polite.

Kade smiled faintly.

That was the tell.

He answered.

"Vance," he said.

"Mr. Vance," the voice replied. Male. Calm. Mid-fifties, maybe. Not rushed. Not rehearsed. Not trying to impress.

"This is Daniel Mercer."

Kade waited.

"I'm calling," Mercer continued, "as a professional courtesy."

Kade leaned against the workbench.

"That's generous," he said.

Mercer chuckled softly. "I'm told you appreciate directness."

Kade didn't confirm or deny it.

"I won't waste your time," Mercer said. "I don't represent the FAA. I don't represent the Department of Defense. And I'm not here to tell you to stop doing anything."

Kade's eyes narrowed slightly.

"That's refreshing," he said.

"Yes," Mercer agreed. "That's why this call isn't recorded."

There it was.

Not a threat.

A boundary marker.

Kade glanced toward the hangar doors—wide open, quiet runway beyond, nothing unusual in sight.

"And who do you represent?" he asked.

Mercer paused just long enough to be deliberate.

"I represent people who prefer problems stay small," he said.

Kade nodded.

"So you're early," he replied.

Mercer smiled—Kade could hear it.

"Earlier than oil," Mercer said. "Later than physics."

Kade felt the hum again—not in the airplane this time, but in his chest. Recognition.

"You saw the data," Kade said.

Mercer didn't deny it.

"We noticed a convergence," he said. "Not the flight. The *effect*."

Kade closed his eyes briefly.

"And you called me instead of sending a letter," he said.

"Yes," Mercer replied. "Because letters create records. Records create misunderstandings."

"And phone calls create favors," Kade said.

Mercer laughed quietly.

"Exactly."

Kade shifted his weight.

"So what's the favor?" he asked.

Mercer's tone stayed even.

"Do nothing," he said.

The words landed heavier than any threat could have.

"Nothing?" Kade repeated.

"Nothing new," Mercer clarified. "No additional flights in that regime. No expansion. No demonstrations. No sharing beyond your current circle."

Kade glanced at the Lear.

"And in return?" he asked.

"In return," Mercer said, "nothing happens."

Kade smiled.

"That's a popular offer these days."

"Yes," Mercer agreed. "It's usually accepted."

Kade was quiet for a long moment.

Mercer didn't rush him.

"That's how I know you're not calling this in," Kade said. "You wouldn't bother if you thought this was going away on its own."

Mercer sighed.

"You're perceptive," he said. "Which is why I'm calling you, and not sending someone else."

"Someone else like who?" Kade asked.

Mercer didn't answer directly.

"Mr. Vance," he said instead, "there are discoveries that change industries. And there are discoveries that change *control structures*."

Kade felt Zara's words echo: *This just stopped being a science problem.*

"I'm guessing this is the second kind," Kade said.

"Yes," Mercer replied. "And those don't age well in public."

Kade looked out at the runway again.

"You didn't tell Yeager not to fly faster," he said quietly.

The line went very still.

"That's not relevant," Mercer said carefully.

Kade smiled.

"It always is," he replied.

Mercer exhaled slowly.

"We didn't know what to do with it then," he said. "We do now."

"And what is that?" Kade asked.

"Keep it contained," Mercer said.

Kade nodded.

"And oil?" he asked.

Mercer chuckled. "Oil wants to buy it. Government wants to prevent it from being used against itself."

Kade felt the shape of the board now—clearer than ever.

"And me?" he asked.

Mercer didn't hesitate.

"You're inconvenient," he said. "But manageable. For now."

Kade laughed once, quietly.

"That's honest."

"Yes," Mercer said. "It's also why I'm asking nicely."

Kade leaned back against the workbench, arms crossed.

"Let me ask you something," he said. "If I hadn't taken that second flight... if I'd just kept tinkering in my hangar... would you still be calling?"

Mercer paused.

"No," he said.

"Then we're already past 'nothing,'" Kade replied.

Silence stretched again.

Mercer broke it.

"I don't need you to stop," he said. "I need you to *pause*."

Kade considered that.

"How long?" he asked.

Mercer didn't answer immediately.

"Long enough for us to understand the implications," he said finally.

Kade smiled faintly.

"You had sixty years," he said.

"That was before the world caught up," Mercer replied.

"And now?" Kade asked.

"Now," Mercer said, "people like you exist."

The line went quiet again—not dead, just waiting.

Kade felt Zara approaching before he saw her, the subtle shift in air, the sound of footsteps he trusted.

"What happens if I don't pause?" Kade asked.

Mercer's voice lowered just a fraction.

"Then this becomes a different kind of conversation," he said. "One with more participants."

Kade nodded.

"Appreciate the courtesy," he said.

Mercer smiled audibly.

"We prefer cooperation."

"I'm sure you do," Kade replied.

He ended the call.

Zara was standing a few feet away now, having caught enough of the exchange to read his posture, his breathing, the way the room felt heavier.

"That was government," she said.

"Indirect," Kade replied.

She nodded. "What did they want?"

Kade looked at the Lear—at the machine that had quietly reopened a door no one had meant to unlock.

"They want time," he said.

Zara's jaw tightened.

"And are you giving it to them?" she asked.

Kade shook his head.

"No," he said. "I'm giving them *misdirection*."

Her eyes sharpened.

"Fly low?" she asked.

Kade smiled.

"Fly invisible," he said.

Zara looked at the 210, then back at him.

"They're still watching the sky," she said.

Kade nodded.

"And still ignoring the ground," he replied.

Outside, the afternoon light shifted, shadows lengthening across the tarmac.

The second call had come.

Not as an order.
Not as a threat.

As a warning wrapped in courtesy.

And Kade understood now:

Oil wanted to own him.
Government wanted to pause him.

Neither one wanted the same thing.

Which meant neither one was in control.

Chapter 18

FLY INVISIBLE

They didn't change the airplane.

That was the point.

No new paint. No new antennas. No visible modifications that would trigger a second look from anyone who happened to wander through a hangar or glance at a flight plan.

The 210 stayed exactly what it had always been: an old, honest airplane that smelled faintly of oil and sun-warmed upholstery, the kind of machine no one associated with breakthroughs or billion-dollar consequences.

Kade liked it that way.

"Everyone watches what moves fast," he said, tightening a cowling latch. "Nobody watches what moves familiar."

Zara sat on an upturned crate, tablet resting on her knee, watching baseline data scroll past. No alerts. No flags. No interest.

"They're still focused on altitude and speed," she said. "Same blind spot as before."

Kade smiled faintly.

"Then let's not educate them."

They flew just after sunrise, when the air was still cool and the sky felt empty. No flight plan worth noticing. No destination worth remembering. Just a meandering route over country so ordinary it barely registered as terrain.

Kade kept the 210 low. Not reckless. Just *present*—a few thousand feet above the ground, slow enough that the world below had time to answer.

The airplane felt different down here.

Not dramatic. Not tense.

Alive.

Zara watched her screen as the first patterns began to form—not sharp, not resolved, but unmistakably coherent.

"It's weaker," she said. "But it's consistent."

Kade nodded. "Like a whisper instead of a shout."

"Yes," she said. "But whispers carry when you know how to listen."

They crossed from hard ground into softer earth and the signal shifted subtly—less organized, more diffuse. Then they skimmed the edge of a dry lake bed and the coherence snapped back into place, clean and unmistakable.

Zara sat forward.

"There," she said. "That transition."

Kade felt it too—not in his hands, not in the controls, but in the way the airplane seemed to settle, as if it had found a rhythm it preferred.

"This is why they missed it," Zara said. "It doesn't look like data. It looks like noise."

She split the display into layers—Lear data from altitude, 210 data from below, historical seismic records stitched together like a quilt of half-truths.

The overlay aligned.

Not perfectly.

But enough to be undeniable.

"This isn't just sensing," she said quietly. "It's *interrogation*."

Kade glanced over. "Say that again."

She hesitated, choosing her words.

"We're not passively observing the ground," she said. "The pressure wave is asking a question. The ground answers differently depending on what's underneath."

Kade swallowed.

"Like ultrasound," he said.

Zara nodded. "Exactly."

They flew on, slow and deliberate, the 210 droning steadily, unremarkable to anyone watching from below—or above.

No one was watching.

That was the beauty of it.

Back in the hangar, they spread the data across multiple screens, cross-checking against public maps, old drilling reports, forgotten surveys.

The picture sharpened.

Not a photograph.

A *truth*.

Zara leaned back, eyes wide now.

"This works anywhere," she said. "As long as you know how to fly the question."

Kade smiled.

"And they're all still watching the sky for answers," he said.

Zara nodded.

"That won't last," she said. "Someone will adapt."

"Someone always does," Kade agreed.

He looked at the 210—Frank's old airplane, still wearing the dust of decades, still doing exactly what it had always done.

Fly.

"Until then," he said, "we stay boring."

Zara laughed softly. "You're terrible at boring."

"Only when it matters," Kade replied.

Outside, the sun climbed higher, the day warming, the world continuing on exactly as it always had—unaware that something fundamental had just slipped beneath its notice.

They hadn't broken any rules.

They hadn't crossed any lines.

They had simply learned how to see without being seen.

And for now, that was enough.

Chapter 19

THE BLIND SPOT CLOSES

The blind spot didn't disappear.

It narrowed.

That was the mistake everyone made when they talked about surveillance—assuming it was a net that either existed or didn't. In reality, it behaved more like eyesight. It adapted. It learned. It compensated.

And when it couldn't see something directly, it learned to look *around* it.

Zara noticed the shift first.

Not in the sky.

In the silence.

She was sitting in the hangar late again, lights low, the kind of hour where systems talked more freely because fewer people were listening. The 210's last flight data scrolled past on one screen, the Lear's earlier runs ghosted on another.

Nothing flagged.

That was the problem.

"Kade," she said.

He was leaning against the Ford's tailgate, nursing a cup of coffee that had gone cold a while ago.

"What?" he asked.

"The access patterns changed."

He straightened. "How?"

Zara rotated her laptop toward him.

"Fewer queries," she said. "But smarter ones."

Kade frowned.

"Meaning?"

"Instead of asking what's under the ground," she said, "they're asking what *changed*."

She pulled up a comparative map—not geological this time, but infrastructural. Power draw anomalies. Fiber routes. Old seismic station locations that were supposed to be dormant.

"They're backing into it," she said. "Using proxies."

Kade exhaled slowly.

"So they still don't see us."

"No," Zara said. "But they see the *absence* of noise where noise should exist."

Kade nodded. "Negative space."

"Exactly."

She highlighted a cluster of points.

"These stations haven't reported anything useful in years," she said. "Now they're being recalibrated."

"By who?" Kade asked.

Zara didn't answer immediately.

She didn't need to.

"Government?" he said.

She nodded. "Not officially. Contractors."

Kade smiled faintly. "That's official enough."

They'd known this moment would come. The second call had made that clear. You could pause a system, misdirect it, slip under it for a while—but eventually, someone noticed the quiet.

Quiet wasn't natural.

Quiet meant something had learned how to hide.

The phone rang again the next morning.

This time it wasn't unknown.

It was a number Kade recognized but hadn't expected to see.

A regional airport manager he'd known for years. A decent man. Careful. Not curious by nature.

"Kade," the man said after the usual pleasantries. "You flying the 210 much lately?"

Kade didn't answer right away.

"Some," he said. "Why?"

There was a pause.

"Got a call," the manager said. "Asking about traffic patterns. Nothing official. Just... odd."

Kade closed his eyes briefly.

"What kind of odd?" he asked.

"They were asking why a certain corridor looks quieter than expected," the man said. "Low-level. General aviation."

Kade nodded slowly.

"And you told them?"

"That I don't track individual pilots," the manager replied. "Because I don't."

"Good," Kade said. "That's still true."

They hung up, and Kade set the phone down carefully, as if sudden movement might make things worse.

"They're triangulating behavior," he said to Zara. "Not speed. Not altitude. Habit."

Zara nodded. "They're looking for the *absence* of randomness."

She pulled up a map of Kade's recent flights, routes crisscrossing like a lazy sketch.

"We're too consistent," she said.

Kade grimaced. "I hate it when you're right."

"We need noise," she continued. "Human noise. Sloppiness. Variation."

Kade smiled slowly.

"Road trips," he said.

Zara blinked. "What?"

"Frank never flew the same way twice unless he had to," Kade said. "Weather, curiosity, boredom—he treated the sky like a suggestion."

Zara's eyes lit up.

"Stochastic flight paths," she said. "Analog randomness."

"Exactly," Kade replied. "We stop flying like a model."

They implemented it immediately.

No repeated routes. No predictable times. Some days they didn't fly at all. Other days they flew just enough to look aimless—touch-and-goes, short hops, errands that meant nothing.

They let the 210 be what it had always been.

A mess.

For a while, it worked.

Then Zara froze again, mid-keystroke.

"They changed again," she said.

Kade looked up. "How?"

"They stopped watching airplanes altogether."

The words landed heavy.

"What do you mean stopped?" he asked.

Zara turned the screen toward him.

"They're watching *us*."

Not visually.

Digitally.

Metadata. Purchases. Power consumption in the hangar. Even the pattern of when the lights were on.

Kade laughed quietly. "That's cheating."

"Yes," Zara agreed. "That's why it works."

She zoomed out, showing the broader pattern.

"They don't know what we're doing," she said. "They just know something important is happening *here*."

Kade leaned back, hands on his hips.

"So the blind spot closed," he said.

Zara nodded. "Not completely. But enough."

Silence settled between them again, thicker now.

Kade walked over to the Lear and rested a hand on its skin.

"They're still afraid of Mach," he said.

"Yes," Zara replied. "Because that's where the old stories live."

Kade smiled faintly.

"Then we don't give them new ones," he said.

Zara looked at him.

"What are you thinking?"

He met her gaze.

"We go public," he said.

Her eyes widened.

"With the tech?" she asked.

"No," Kade said. "With *me*."

She frowned. "Explain."

"I stop being invisible," he said. "I become noise. Speaking gigs. Aviation panels. Old warbird fly-ins. Let them think I'm just another pilot with opinions."

Zara considered it, then nodded slowly.

"Human camouflage," she said.

"And while they're watching *me*," Kade continued, "they stop watching the ground."

Zara smiled.

"That might just work," she said.

Outside, the day carried on—planes taking off, cars passing, systems recalibrating themselves around a problem they still didn't understand.

The blind spot hadn't vanished.

It had shifted.

And Kade intended to shift with it—staying just out of focus, just out of reach, flying not faster or higher...

...but smarter.

Chapter 20

DON'T BREAK MACH

The rule had never been written down.

That was the first thing Kade understood once he stopped looking for it in manuals, regulations, or policy memos. There was no paragraph you could quote. No CFR reference. No official boundary with a name.

Just a consensus.

Unspoken.
Unchallenged.
Absolute.

Don't break Mach.

Not because it was dangerous.
Not because it was noisy.
Not even because it was illegal.

Because it changed who was listening.

Kade stood alone in the Lear's cockpit, canopy open, morning air spilling in, the smell of fuel and metal and old avionics mixing into something that felt familiar enough to be comforting and new enough to be dangerous.

Mach .92.

That number was taped to the side of the instrument panel now. Not as a goal. As a reminder.

He didn't need to go faster. That was the mistake everyone made—assuming revelation required excess. It didn't.

It required **alignment**.

Zara climbed the ladder and stepped into the cockpit, carrying two coffees.

"You're thinking too hard," she said, handing one to him.

"I'm thinking just enough," he replied.

She glanced at the taped number.

"They drew the line there for a reason," she said.

Kade nodded.

"Because it's close enough to taste," he said. "But far enough to pretend it's coincidence."

Zara leaned against the bulkhead.

"Mach one makes headlines," she said. "Mach point nine makes spreadsheets."

"And spreadsheets get buried," Kade replied.

They sat in silence for a moment, the Lear creaking softly as it warmed in the sun.

"Yeager crossed it because that was the challenge," Zara said. "He wanted to prove you could."

"And that's why they noticed," Kade said.

Zara nodded. "Breaking Mach wasn't the discovery. It was the *signal*."

Kade stared out across the runway.

"The mistake wasn't flying faster," he said. "It was flying faster *publicly*."

Zara's eyes sharpened. "Say that again."

"Mach one isn't a physical barrier," Kade said. "It's a social one. Cross it and you trigger mythology. Attention. Ownership."

Zara smiled slowly.

"And Mach .92?" she asked.

Kade smiled back.

"That's where physics speaks quietly enough to be ignored," he said.

They powered up the Lear but didn't start engines. Systems hummed. Screens glowed. Everything ready without anything happening.

"You realize," Zara said, "that the moment you break Mach, the rules change."

"Yes," Kade said. "The moment you *don't*, the rules can't find you."

She took a sip of coffee.

"That's why Mercer said pause," she said. "He wasn't afraid of what you'd see. He was afraid of who else would hear it."

Kade nodded.

"And oil wanted exclusivity because speed scares investors," he said. "But predictability scares governments more."

Zara looked at him carefully.

"You're not going to cross it," she said.

"No," Kade replied. "I'm going to *use* it."

She frowned slightly. "Explain."

"Mach one is a decoy," Kade said. "Everyone thinks the secret lives there. The truth is the regime just below it—the transition. The conversation between air and ground."

Zara's breath caught.

"That's why Yeager felt it *before* he broke through," she said.

"Yes," Kade replied. "He heard the whisper. Then everyone focused on the bang."

They shut the Lear down and climbed out without ever leaving the ground.

Outside, a Gulfstream lifted off smoothly, climbing hard, accelerating confidently toward the upper limits of what was allowed and celebrated.

Mach .90.
Mach .92.
Mach .94.

Close enough to be admired.

Not close enough to matter.

Kade watched it disappear into the haze.

"They're still daring people to cross it," he said.

Zara nodded. "Because as long as no one does, the myth holds."

Kade turned back to the hangar, to the 210, to the tools and screens and quiet machines that didn't care about myths.

"We don't break Mach," he said again. "Ever."

Zara smiled.

"That's the rule," she said.

"And the advantage," Kade replied.

She met his gaze.

"So what happens when someone else crosses it?" she asked.

Kade didn't answer right away.

Because that question had only one ending.

"When someone else breaks Mach," he said finally, "they'll light themselves up like a flare."

Zara nodded slowly.

"And we'll already know what they just revealed," she said.

Kade smiled faintly.

"Exactly."

The rule wasn't about speed.

It was about **who controlled the narrative**.

And as long as Kade stayed just below the line everyone watched, he could hear everything without ever being heard.

Mach one was the loudest lie in aviation.

And he had no intention of proving it wrong.

Chapter 21

NOISE

Kade didn't announce anything.

That was the mistake people expected him to make—press releases, big reveals, cryptic posts that drew the wrong kind of attention. Instead, he did something far more effective.

He became *ordinary* in public.

The first panel was in Phoenix. An aviation safety symposium with bad coffee, worse name badges, and a room full of people who liked the sound of their own voices. Kade sat in the second row, boots crossed at the ankles, listening to arguments about noise abatement and next-generation avionics like they were religious debates.

He raised his hand exactly once.

"What's your take on high-subsonic regimes?" he asked, voice calm, curious, forgettable.

The panelist—an engineer with three degrees and no flight time—gave a safe answer. Numbers. Compliance. Margins.

Kade nodded, thanked him, and didn't follow up.

Zara watched from the back of the room, smiling faintly.

"That was perfect," she said afterward.

"I didn't say anything," Kade replied.

"Exactly."

The second appearance was louder.

A warbird fly-in outside San Antonio. Old jets. Old men. Old stories. Kade wandered the flight line in jeans and a faded jacket, answering questions about restoration projects, laughing at the right moments, telling stories about the 210 like it was the only airplane he'd ever loved.

Someone asked about the Lear.

"Old muscle car," Kade said. "Fun to tinker with. Drinks fuel like it's free."

No one wrote that down.

That night, he posted a photo online—him leaning against Frank's old Ford, sunset behind the hangar, the caption simple:

Nothing beats keeping old machines alive.

The post got likes. Comments. Nothing else.

Which was the point.

By the third week, Kade was everywhere and nowhere at once.

Aviation podcasts. Industry lunches. Panel discussions where nothing of substance was ever said. He talked about safety. About analog skills. About how modern pilots relied too much on automation.

He never mentioned Mach.

Never mentioned pressure waves.

Never mentioned mapping.

And because he was visible, because he was *predictable*, the systems adjusted around him.

Zara showed him the metrics late one night, the glow of screens lighting the hangar walls.

"They've widened the aperture," she said. "Less focus. More noise tolerance."

Kade nodded. "Good."

"They think you're harmless," she added.

Kade smiled faintly.

"That's usually when people stop looking at what you're doing," he said.

They flew less during that period. Or rather, they flew *messier*. Short hops. Odd hours. Routes that went nowhere and meant nothing.

The 210 became a prop in a different performance now—one of normalcy.

And while eyes tracked Kade the *person*, no one tracked the data.

That was the trade.

Until the email arrived.

Not to Kade.

To Zara.

Subject: **Invitation — Closed-Door Briefing**

No sender listed. No organization. Just a date, a city, and a sentence that tightened the room instantly.

We believe your work may intersect with emerging aerospace and energy considerations.

Zara stared at it, then looked up at Kade.

"They're trying to bring us inside," she said.

Kade nodded. "That means they're uncomfortable."

"They want context," she said. "Control."

"They want to see if we'll talk," Kade replied.

Zara exhaled slowly.

"And if we don't?"

Kade shrugged.

"Then someone else will," he said. "And they'll say the wrong thing."

He walked to the Lear, ran a hand along the fuselage like he was checking a horse before a long ride.

"Noise works until it doesn't," he said. "Eventually, silence becomes suspicious again."

Zara leaned against the workbench.

"So what's the move?"

Kade smiled—not wide, not reckless. Just enough.

"We accept," he said. "But we don't bring the truth."

Zara raised an eyebrow. "We lie?"

"No," Kade said. "We give them something louder."

She understood instantly.

A decoy.

A version of the story that fit inside their expectations.

"That's dangerous," she said.

"So is letting them invent their own," Kade replied.

Outside, a jet roared overhead—loud, visible, admired.

Noise.

Kade watched it pass, then turned back to the quiet machines in the hangar.

"They think the threat is speed," he said.

Zara nodded. "And spectacle."

Kade smiled.

"Then that's what we give them," he said. "Just enough to keep them busy."

Zara closed her laptop, eyes sharp now.

"And while they listen to the noise," she said, "we keep listening to the ground."

Kade nodded.

Noise wasn't chaos.

Noise was cover.

And in a world obsessed with breaking barriers loudly, Kade had found a far more effective way to move unseen —

By letting everyone think they could hear him.

Chapter 22

THE FIRST MISTAKE

It wasn't arrogance that did it.

Everyone liked to believe mistakes came from ego, from bravado, from someone thinking they were smarter than the system. That made the story cleaner. Moral. Safe.

This one came from impatience.

The jet lifted out of Nevada just after dawn, climbing hard, clean, confident. Experimental registration. Private money. Former military test pilots in the cockpit, the kind of men who'd spent their lives on the right side of classified and had learned to trust that the system always told you when you'd gone too far.

They believed the silence meant permission.

Zara saw it first.

Not the jet itself—no transponder alert, no public feed. She saw the *ripple*. A sudden tightening across multiple datasets that had no business talking to each other.

She froze.

"Kade," she said.

He looked up from the workbench immediately. "What?"

"Someone just lit the sky," she replied.

She pulled the feeds up side by side. Atmospheric sensors. Pressure arrays. Old acoustic stations that had been "inactive" for years.

All of them reacted at once.

Not noise.

Coherence.

Kade leaned in, eyes narrowing.

"They crossed it," he said.

Zara nodded slowly.

"Mach one," she said. "Clean. Over land."

Kade exhaled through his nose.

"Damn."

The data bloomed outward like a shockwave—but not the kind the public imagined. No shattered windows. No sonic boom reports lighting up social media.

This was different.

This was *structural*.

The patterns tightened, aligned, then snapped into something unmistakable before dissolving again into noise.

Zara's hands moved fast now, capturing everything before anyone thought to delete it.

"They didn't just break Mach," she said. "They broke *containment*."

Kade stared at the screen.

The ground response was violent in its clarity—layers exposed, boundaries flaring briefly like bones under an X-ray before vanishing again.

"Too loud," he said.

"Yes," Zara replied. "Too fast. Too public."

Phones started ringing across the hangar—not Kade's. Zara's secure line lit up first, then went dark. Then lit again.

"Everyone felt that," she said.

Kade nodded.

"They rang the bell," he said. "And bells don't unring."

Within minutes, the world began to react—but sideways, the way institutions always did when something happened they didn't understand.

Airspace advisories.
Environmental reviews.
Sudden "maintenance" outages at monitoring stations.

A scramble.

Zara watched the responses cascade, lips pressed into a thin line.

"They're trying to stuff it back into the box," she said.

"Too late," Kade replied.

The data was already copied. Already mirrored. Already understood by people who didn't need permission to recognize what they were seeing.

"Who was it?" Kade asked.

Zara pulled up a name.

A startup. Well-funded. Loud. Publicly obsessed with breaking barriers and rewriting aviation history.

"Of course," Kade said. "They wanted headlines."

"And investors," Zara added.

Kade shook his head.

"They thought speed was the story," he said.

Zara looked up at him.

"It always is—until it isn't."

The first public explanation came fast.

Unusual atmospheric conditions.
Test flight anomaly.
No threat to public safety.

The language was careful. Reassuring.

And completely beside the point.

Kade watched it all unfold from the quiet of his hangar, Frank's old truck parked outside, the 210 sitting patiently like it always had.

"They broke the rule," he said.

Zara nodded. "And proved it exists."

She pulled up the Lear's earlier data, overlaid with the new spike from the supersonic run.

The contrast was brutal.

Kade's work was subtle. Surgical. Invisible unless you knew where to look.

The other flight was a flare.

Bright enough for everyone to see—and bright enough to burn.

Zara leaned back, exhausted now.

"They'll blame the tech," she said. "Or the pilot. Or the weather."

"They won't blame the truth," Kade replied.

"No," she agreed. "They never do."

Outside, a jet passed overhead—ordinary, loud, celebrated.

Kade didn't look up.

"Now the pressure changes," he said.

Zara nodded. "Now they start closing doors."

Kade smiled faintly.

"Good," he said. "They always reveal more when they panic."

Zara met his gaze.

"And us?"

Kade glanced at the Lear, then at the 210.

"We stay exactly where we are," he said. "Just below the line."

Zara exhaled slowly.

"They broke Mach," she said.

Kade nodded.

"And told the world where *not* to look," he replied.

Silence settled again—heavy, charged, inevitable.

The first mistake had been made.

Not by Kade.

By someone who thought speed was the goal.

Chapter 23

THE FLARE

The flare burned longer than anyone expected.

Not in the sky—that part was over in seconds—but in the systems that watched the sky, the ground, and everything in between. What the jet had ignited wasn't outrage or panic. It was *attention*. The kind that couldn't be turned off once it latched on.

By noon, the story had fractured into a dozen versions.

Experimental aircraft exceeds expectations.
Unusual atmospheric event recorded over Nevada.
Data anomaly prompts review.

Each headline said something different. None of them said the right thing.

Kade watched it all from the hangar, phone face-down on the workbench, the radio murmuring half-formed explanations that sounded confident until you listened closely.

Zara stood beside him, scrolling.

"They're flooding the zone," she said.

"Always do," Kade replied. "Noise to drown out signal."

The startup's CEO appeared on a financial network, smiling too much, talking about innovation and progress, assuring investors that nothing had gone wrong—*nothing at all*—just a successful test that had been "misinterpreted by automated systems."

Automated systems.

Zara snorted. "They're blaming the listeners."

Kade nodded. "That's step one."

Behind the scenes, it was worse.

Airspace corridors shifted without explanation. Research flights were quietly canceled. Data repositories went dark for "scheduled maintenance" that hadn't been scheduled.

Zara pulled up a map of monitoring stations.

"They're shutting down everything that spiked," she said. "Trying to erase the flare after it already lit the room."

Kade leaned back against the Lear.

"Too late," he said. "You can't unring a bell, and you can't unsee a pattern."

Zara's screen chimed softly.

"Here we go," she said.

Another invitation. Another closed-door briefing. Different city. Different sponsor. Same language.

We'd value your perspective.

"They're widening the net," she said. "Trying to figure out who else knows."

Kade smiled faintly.

"And assuming the loudest people matter most."

Zara nodded. "They always do."

That afternoon, a call came—not to Kade, not to Zara, but to a journalist Kade knew by reputation. Aviation. Serious. Old-school. The kind who still read accident reports for fun.

Zara listened on speaker as the man spoke, voice cautious.

"Off the record," he said. "Did you feel that?"

Zara glanced at Kade.

"Feel what?" she asked.

"The data shift," the journalist replied. "It's like something tapped the glass from the inside."

Kade closed his eyes briefly.

"That's poetic," he said when Zara relayed it.

"It's dangerous," she replied.

Because journalists didn't talk like that unless they were already circling something real.

By evening, the official explanation solidified.

A joint statement. Carefully worded. Comforting.

No evidence of sustained supersonic operations over land.
No public safety risk.
No new regulatory considerations at this time.

Zara read it twice.

"They're lying by omission," she said.

Kade shrugged. "That's still lying."

Outside, the sun dipped low, casting the runway in gold. Planes took off and landed like they always had. Life continued.

But the flare had done its job.

Inside secure rooms, people replayed the data. Argued over interpretations. Pointed fingers. Asked the wrong questions loudly and the right ones quietly.

Zara shut her laptop and looked at Kade.

"They're scared," she said.

Kade nodded. "They should be."

"Not of speed," she added.

"Of losing the map," he replied.

They stood there together, listening to the hum of systems cooling, the distant sound of a jet departing—loud, proud, irrelevant.

The flare had drawn every eye upward.

Which meant no one was looking at the ground anymore.

Kade broke the silence.

"They think this is about controlling aircraft," he said.

Zara smiled faintly. "And it's really about controlling knowledge."

Kade nodded.

"And knowledge," he said, "has a habit of moving sideways when you try to trap it."

Zara met his gaze.

"What now?" she asked.

Kade looked at the Lear, then the 210, then Frank's old truck—three machines that didn't care about headlines or committees.

"Now," he said, "we let them chase the light."

Zara smiled.

"And we keep the truth in the dark," she said.

The flare would fade.

The noise would settle.

But the pattern had already been seen by the wrong people—and understood by the right ones.

And somewhere, beneath the arguments and press releases and reassurances, the ground waited.

Ready to answer again.

Chapter 24

QUIET DATA

The most dangerous data never announced itself.

It didn't spike.
It didn't flare.
It didn't demand attention.

It sat.

Waiting for someone patient enough to understand what it already knew.

Kade and Zara didn't talk much the morning after the flare. There was nothing left to say about what had happened. The world had reacted exactly the way Kade expected it to—loudly, defensively, and in all the wrong directions.

The hangar felt different now. Not tense. Focused.

Zara stood at the main workstation, sleeves rolled up, hair pulled back, the kind of posture she slipped into when the outside world no longer mattered. Multiple screens glowed softly, each showing a different slice of the same truth.

Lear data.
210 data.
Public seismic surveys.
Private anomalies scraped quietly from places no one thought to lock down yet.

Kade watched from a few feet away, coffee untouched, Maggie asleep under the wing like she always was when everything felt right.

"They're all chasing the flare," Zara said without looking up.

Kade nodded. "That's what flares are for."

She pulled up a composite view—nothing flashy, nothing dramatic. Just layers aligning in ways they weren't supposed to.

"This," she said, tapping the screen, "is what they don't have."

Kade stepped closer.

It wasn't a map.

It was a **conversation**.

Pressure responses stitched across geography. Density shifts that didn't belong to nature alone. Subsurface geometries that revealed intent—human fingerprints written in stone and soil.

Zara zoomed in on a section.

"They hid this by averaging," she said. "By smoothing. By making everything look natural enough to pass."

Kade leaned in.

"And we didn't," he said.

"No," she replied. "We listened."

The quiet data told a different story than the flare ever could. Where the supersonic event had shouted once and disappeared, this spoke continuously—softly, insistently, impossible to erase without erasing entire systems.

Zara highlighted a region.

"This wasn't built to be secret forever," she said. "It was built to be secret until no one remembered how to look."

Kade felt that land.

Not metaphorically. Physically.

The same way he'd felt the hum at Mach .92.

"So the danger isn't exposure," he said. "It's comprehension."

Zara nodded.

"Exactly," she said. "Anyone can see the flare. Only a few people can understand *this*."

She leaned back, rubbing her eyes.

"They can shut down sensors," she continued. "They can rewrite reports. They can intimidate pilots and buy startups."

She looked at him now.

"But they can't uninvent the physics."

Kade smiled faintly.

"That's always been their blind spot."

Zara pulled up another screen—an archive she'd been building quietly since Yeager's logbook.

Dates.
Flights.
Policy shifts.
Seismic suppression.
Funding reallocations.

A pattern stretching across decades.

"They didn't stop supersonic flight because of noise," she said. "They stopped it because the ground started answering questions they didn't know how to control."

Kade nodded.

"And now," he said, "we know how to ask better questions."

Silence settled again—not heavy this time, but complete.

The work was done.

Not finished.
But finished enough.

Zara closed the final file and encrypted it twice—not because she feared theft, but because some things deserved friction.

"They're going to come back," she said.

Kade nodded. "With better offers."

"And worse consequences."

"Yes."

She met his gaze.

"What do *we* do?" she asked.

Kade looked around the hangar—the Lear resting quietly, the 210 still dusty from yesterday's flight, Frank's old truck outside exactly where it had always been.

"We don't sell," he said.

Zara nodded.

"We don't publish," he added.

She hesitated. "Yet."

"Yet," he agreed.

He walked over to the whiteboard and erased everything except one phrase Zara had written weeks ago and never removed.

MEASURE, DON'T FILTER

Kade underlined it.

"They can control speed," he said. "They can control noise."

He turned back to her.

"They can't control *understanding*."

Zara smiled slowly.

"And understanding," she said, "moves faster than any airplane."

Outside, another jet roared overhead—loud, proud, celebrated.

Inside, the truth sat quietly on encrypted drives, already complete, already patient.

The flare had been a warning.

The quiet data was the weapon.

And for the first time since this all began, Kade felt something settle in his chest—not fear, not excitement.

Certainty.

They were already ahead.

Chapter 25

THE OFFER REWRITTEN

The third offer arrived without a phone call.

That alone told Kade everything he needed to know.

No voice meant no favors.
No favors meant alignment.

Oil and government didn't like each other, but they understood one thing perfectly: when something threatened *both* of them, it was better to sit at the same table than pretend the table didn't exist.

The envelope showed up mid-morning. Hand-delivered. No return address. Thick paper. Expensive in the way that never tried to look expensive.

Zara turned it over twice before opening it.

"No logo," she said. "No letterhead."

Kade nodded. "That's on purpose."

Inside was a single sheet and a business card—blank except for a name and a number.

Caleb Rhodes
Daniel Mercer

No titles. No companies.

Just two men who had already tried separately—and failed.

Zara read the letter out loud.

Mr. Vance,
Recent events have clarified the scope of your work. We believe continued parallel efforts introduce unnecessary risk.
Accordingly, we propose a coordinated framework to ensure stability, discretion, and mutual benefit.
Terms available upon discussion.

Zara looked up.

"They didn't say partnership," she said.

"They didn't say purchase," Kade replied.

"They didn't say stop," she added.

Kade smiled faintly.

"They said *framework*," he said. "That's the word people use when they want control without fingerprints."

Zara flipped the page.

"Meeting location," she said. "Neutral ground. Private airstrip. No devices."

"Of course," Kade said.

Zara didn't sit down.

"This is escalation," she said. "They're done circling."

"Yes," Kade replied. "Now they're closing the box."

She hesitated.

"And if we don't go?"

Kade leaned against the workbench, arms folded.

"Then they'll decide for us," he said. "Or decide we're the problem."

Zara nodded slowly.

"So we go," she said.

Kade smiled.

"But not to negotiate," he said.

Zara raised an eyebrow. "Then why?"

Kade met her gaze.

"To redefine the terms."

The airstrip was exactly what it was supposed to be.

Too clean. Too quiet. Too forgettable.

No signage. No cameras anyone could admit to. Just a strip of asphalt in the middle of nothing, surrounded by scrub and distance.

Kade flew the 210 in himself.

Slow. Ordinary. Invisible.

A black SUV waited at the far end of the ramp, engine running, windows dark. Another sat farther back—not for them, just to be seen.

Zara didn't comment.

They were led into a low building that smelled faintly of coffee and recycled air. A conference room waited inside—glass table, four chairs, water already poured.

Rhodes stood first. Mercer followed a beat later.

They shook hands like men who had agreed not to remember each other's pasts.

"Mr. Vance," Rhodes said. "Ms. Quinn."

Zara didn't correct him on her last name.

Mercer gestured toward the chairs.

"Thank you for coming," he said. "We'll keep this efficient."

Kade sat, relaxed, boots planted, hands open on the table.

"That's usually code for 'decided already,'" he said.

Rhodes smiled. "We prefer to think of it as aligned."

Mercer slid a tablet across the table. Screen dark.

"Before we begin," he said, "I want to be clear. This conversation doesn't exist."

Kade nodded. "That makes three of us."

Mercer tapped the screen.

"Your technology," he said, "represents a non-traditional sensing capability with profound implications for national security and resource stability."

Zara leaned back slightly.

"That's a long way of saying you don't control it," she said.

Rhodes didn't flinch.

"Not yet," he replied.

Mercer continued.

"We propose the following," he said. "You retain authorship. We retain oversight. Applications proceed through approved channels only."

Kade smiled faintly.

"And in return?" he asked.

Rhodes leaned forward.

"Immunity," he said. "Funding. Protection."

Zara laughed once—soft, humorless.

"From who?" she asked.

Rhodes met her eyes.

"From us," he said.

Silence settled.

Kade studied them both—the oil man who thought in acreage and influence, the government man who thought in decades and denial.

They weren't evil.

They were afraid.

"You rewrote the offer," Kade said.

"Yes," Mercer replied. "We had to."

Kade nodded slowly.

"And here's the problem," he said. "You're still offering me something I already have."

Rhodes frowned slightly. "Control?"

Kade shook his head.

"Time," he said.

Mercer stiffened.

"You don't have time," he said. "Not anymore."

Kade leaned forward now, voice calm, almost gentle.

"I already finished," he said.

The room went very still.

Zara didn't move.

Rhodes' smile vanished.

"What do you mean finished?" Mercer asked.

Kade met his gaze.

"The data exists," he said. "The model exists. The understanding exists."

He leaned back again.

"You're not negotiating access," he continued. "You're negotiating *when* you find out how far behind you are."

Mercer closed his eyes briefly.

Rhodes exhaled through his nose.

"This doesn't have to become adversarial," Rhodes said.

Kade nodded. "It already is."

Silence stretched.

Then Mercer spoke quietly.

"What do you want, Mr. Vance?"

Kade didn't answer immediately.

He thought of Yeager.
Of Frank.
Of the ground answering questions it had never been asked politely before.

"I want it used," he said. "Not owned."

Zara looked at him.

"Open," Mercer said sharply. "That's impossible."

Kade shook his head.

"Selective," he said. "Transparent. Auditable."

Rhodes scoffed. "That destroys leverage."

"Yes," Kade replied. "That's the point."

Mercer studied him for a long moment.

"You're asking us to give up control," he said.

Kade smiled faintly.

"You already lost it," he replied. "You just haven't accepted it yet."

They sat in silence, the offer rewritten again—this time not on paper, but in power.

Finally, Mercer stood.

"We'll need time," he said.

Kade nodded. "You always do."

Rhodes remained seated, eyes cold now.

"You're betting everything on being right," he said.

Kade met his gaze.

"No," he replied. "I'm betting everything on physics."

They stood. No hands were shaken this time.

As Kade and Zara walked back toward the 210, Zara let out a slow breath.

"That was... nuclear," she said.

Kade smiled.

"They came to close the box," he said. "They left knowing it never belonged to them."

Zara glanced back at the building.

"What happens now?" she asked.

Kade started the engine, the old Continental rumbling to life.

"Now," he said, "they decide whether to adapt... or escalate."

The 210 rolled forward, lifted off, and vanished into the ordinary sky.

Behind them, two men sat in a room designed to forget conversations, staring at a future they could no longer schedule.

Chapter 26

THE MAP NO ONE ASKED FOR

They didn't intend to build it.

That was the part that bothered Kade the most.

The map emerged the way real discoveries always did—not as a goal, not as a deliverable, but as a side effect of asking better questions than anyone else had thought to ask before.

Zara noticed it late at night, long after the hangar should have been quiet. She was running a cross-domain pass—one last integrity check before archiving the day's work—when the system hesitated.

Not crashed.

Hesitated.

She froze, hands hovering over the keyboard.

"Kade," she said softly.

He looked up from the workbench. "What did it do?"

"It didn't fail," she said. "It... reorganized."

She rotated the screen toward him.

At first glance, it looked like noise. A chaotic tangle of lines and gradients that didn't belong to any traditional representation—no lat-long grid, no depth scale, no clean labels.

Then Kade tilted his head.

"I see it," he said.

Zara nodded.

"The system stopped trying to answer the question we were asking," she said. "And started answering the one underneath it."

She zoomed out.

The image stabilized—not into a geological map, not into an infrastructure diagram, but into something stranger and far more unsettling.

A **negative space map**.

"What's missing," Kade said.

"Yes," Zara replied. "Not what's there. What *isn't*."

They stared at it together.

Entire regions—supposedly ordinary land—showed subtle but consistent absences. Places where pressure responses should have scattered but didn't. Where the ground behaved as if it were hollowed, reinforced, altered.

Not random.

Intentional.

"This wasn't designed to be found," Zara said.

"No," Kade replied. "It was designed to be *ignored*."

She pulled up public records over the same areas—zoning maps, environmental assessments, infrastructure plans. Everything looked normal.

Too normal.

"They flattened it," she said. "Made the averages lie."

Kade felt the hum again—not physical this time, but cognitive. The sensation of a pattern snapping into place.

"This isn't oil infrastructure," he said.

Zara shook her head. "Oil hides underground because it has to. This hides because it *chooses* to."

She toggled a different layer.

The map sharpened.

Kade inhaled slowly.

"Logistics," he said. "Connectivity."

Zara nodded. "Movement without visibility."

The implications settled like weight in the room.

"This explains the suppression," Zara said. "The policy. The noise obsession. Mach as a myth."

Kade nodded.

"They didn't care about sonic booms," he said. "They cared about mapping."

Zara leaned back in her chair.

"And once this existed," she said, "supersonic flight over land became unacceptable."

Because supersonic flight wasn't loud.

It was *revealing*.

They sat in silence, the map glowing softly between them, showing a world that had been carefully edited for decades.

"No one asked for this," Zara said quietly.

Kade nodded.

"And that's why it matters," he replied.

The map didn't accuse. It didn't explain. It simply *existed*—an unavoidable answer to a question no one in power wanted asked.

Zara closed the file without saving it under any obvious name.

"What do we call it?" she asked.

Kade thought for a moment.

"Nothing," he said. "It doesn't get a name yet."

She smiled faintly. "Smart."

Because names invited ownership.

They encrypted the data and separated it—pieces stored in places that didn't know about each other, fragments useless on their own.

Not paranoia.

Redundancy.

Kade leaned against the Lear, arms crossed, staring at the white fuselage like it was an old friend who'd just told him something he couldn't forget.

"This is why they're afraid," he said.

Zara nodded. "This doesn't just show what's underground."

"It shows where the lies are," Kade finished.

Outside, the hangar doors stood open, the night air cool and still. No sirens. No calls. No pressure.

Yet.

"This changes how the world works," Zara said.

Kade shook his head.

"No," he said. "It changes how the world *can* work."

He looked back at the map one last time before shutting down the screens.

"And that's always worse."

The map no one asked for was complete—not finished, not polished, but undeniable.

Somewhere, decisions had been made decades ago to hide certain questions beneath layers of policy and noise and speed limits.

Kade had just peeled those layers back.

Not with force.

With understanding.

And the most dangerous thing about the map wasn't what it showed.

It was that once seen, it couldn't be unseen.

Chapter 27

TIMING

Timing was the part no one respected anymore.

Speed had replaced it. Urgency. The belief that if you didn't act immediately, you'd lose your window forever. That was how people talked themselves into mistakes—by convincing themselves that hesitation was weakness.

Kade knew better.

He'd learned it flying weather. Learned it landing on short strips with no go-around. Learned it watching men with too much money rush into deals they didn't understand and spend years paying for the hurry.

Timing wasn't about *when* something happened.

It was about when it **couldn't be stopped**.

The map sat dormant now—broken into fragments, encrypted, quiet. Not hidden, exactly. Just patient. Like something that knew it didn't need to announce itself to be real.

Zara leaned against the workbench, arms folded, eyes on the blank screens.

"They're waiting," she said.

"Yes," Kade replied. "So are we."

Outside, the hangar doors were open, the afternoon light steady and unremarkable. The kind of day that made urgency feel unnecessary—dangerous even.

Zara glanced at him.

"You're not worried," she said.

"I am," Kade replied. "Just not about the same things they are."

She smiled faintly.

"They're worried about exposure," she said.

"And I'm worried about *misuse*," he said.

That was the difference.

They'd crossed the point where the discovery could be buried again. Too many systems had already brushed against it. Too many professionals had felt the improvement, the tightening, the way their models suddenly behaved better without explanation.

The toothpaste wasn't going back in the tube.

But that didn't mean you squeezed it out recklessly.

Zara pulled up a calendar—not dates, not deadlines, but **conditions**.

Public distraction cycles.
Election noise.
Market volatility.
Regulatory bandwidth.

"This is when the system is loudest," she said, highlighting blocks of time. "And least capable of subtle response."

Kade nodded.

"You don't move during calm," he said. "You move during storms."

Zara met his gaze.

"And if they escalate first?" she asked.

Kade shrugged.

"Then they reveal their hand," he said. "Escalation always costs more than patience."

He walked over to the Lear, resting a hand on its skin like he'd done a hundred times before.

"They still think this is about control," he said.

Zara nodded. "And control needs something to push against."

Kade smiled faintly.

"So we don't push," he said. "We wait."

Silence settled again—not heavy, not anxious. Deliberate.

The kind of silence that existed because nothing needed to happen yet.

Zara broke it.

"What's the trigger?" she asked.

Kade thought for a moment.

"Second-order use," he said.

She frowned. "Explain."

"When someone else tries to *apply* it," he said. "Not study it. Not suppress it. Use it."

Zara's eyes widened slightly.

"That's when the risk becomes obvious," she said.

"And unavoidable," Kade replied.

He turned back to the whiteboard and wrote a single word:

INEVITABLE

"You don't announce inevitability," he said. "You let people discover it when it's too late to pretend it isn't there."

Zara stared at the word.

"So timing isn't about publishing," she said slowly.

"No," Kade agreed. "It's about *alignment*."

With markets.
With politics.
With consequences.

The phone didn't ring that day.

Neither did it the next.

That, more than anything, told Kade they were doing it right.

Because silence from power meant calculation.

And calculation meant uncertainty.

Zara packed up for the night, pausing at the hangar door.

"They're going to move the line again," she said.

Kade nodded.

"They always do."

"And when they do?" she asked.

Kade smiled—not reckless, not eager. Ready.

"We move with it," he said. "Just ahead. Always just ahead."

Outside, the sun dipped low, shadows stretching long across the runway. A jet climbed into the sky, loud and fast and watched by everyone who still believed speed was the story.

Kade didn't look up.

Timing wasn't about being first.

It was about being *impossible to ignore*—at exactly the wrong moment for the people who wanted you quiet.

And that moment was coming.

Not fast.

Not slow.

Right on time.

Chapter 28

THE LINE MOVES

They didn't announce the change.

They never did.

Lines didn't move with press conferences or signatures anymore. They moved through guidance memos, updated definitions, quiet revisions to words that looked harmless until you realized what they replaced.

Zara caught it on a Tuesday morning.

Not because she was looking for it—but because she always read the footnotes.

"Kade," she said.

He was in the hangar, one hand inside the Lear's avionics bay, the other resting casually on the edge of the panel like this was just another maintenance day.

"What did they call it this time?" he asked.

She turned her screen toward him.

INTERIM GUIDANCE — TRANSONIC OPERATIONS
Clarification of 'Sustained Supersonic'

Zara scrolled.

The language was careful. Almost elegant.

Supersonic flight was still prohibited over land— *sustained* supersonic flight. A subtle distinction, newly emphasized. A paragraph buried deep enough that only lawyers and engineers would ever notice.

"They redefined the word," Zara said.

Kade nodded.

"They always do," he replied.

The new guidance didn't mention Mach one directly. It didn't need to. Instead, it talked about *duration*, *persistence*, *intent*. Short excursions were still violations—technically—but enforcement language softened around "brief transonic anomalies."

Anomalies.

Zara laughed quietly.

"They just made room for the flare," she said.

Kade leaned back, wiping his hands.

"And closed the door behind it," he said.

Because the line hadn't moved *up*.

It had moved *sideways*.

The public story remained intact: supersonic flight over land was still forbidden. Noise still mattered. Safety still mattered.

But in the margins, the system had adjusted—making what had just happened an exception, not a precedent.

"They're containing it," Zara said.

"Yes," Kade replied. "And acknowledging it at the same time."

She frowned.

"That's not sustainable," she said.

"No," Kade agreed. "It's reactive."

The second indicator came later that afternoon.

A canceled symposium. Quietly removed from the schedule. No explanation. Just gone.

The title had been innocuous enough:

Advances in Subsurface Sensing and Remote Interrogation

Zara stared at the archived page.

"They killed it," she said.

"Too soon," Kade replied.

"They're slowing the conversation," she added.

"Yes," he said. "Which means the conversation exists."

Power didn't slow things that weren't real.

By evening, the third sign arrived.

A procurement notice—public, but vague. Funding allocated for "environmental modeling enhancements" and "non-invasive ground response characterization."

Zara leaned back in her chair.

"That's our language," she said.

Kade nodded.

"They're trying to build it themselves," he said.

"And they're late," she added.

Kade smiled faintly.

"They're always late," he said. "They wait for permission."

The line had moved.

Not in altitude.
Not in speed.

In *ownership*.

What had once been forbidden was now "under review."
What had once been dismissed was now "under study."
What had once been ignored was now being quietly replicated by institutions that hated nothing more than discovering they'd missed something.

"They can't stop it," Zara said.

"No," Kade replied. "They can only decide who pretends to discover it next."

Zara met his gaze.

"And us?"

Kade walked to the whiteboard and erased the word **INEVITABLE**.

He wrote a new one beneath it.

DOCUMENTED

"They'll try to claim it," he said. "We don't fight that."

Zara frowned slightly.

"Then what do we do?"

Kade capped the marker.

"We make it undeniable," he said. "And boring."

She blinked. "Boring?"

"Yes," he replied. "Once something becomes boring, it stops being controllable."

Zara smiled slowly.

"Like GPS," she said. "Or the internet."

"Exactly," Kade replied.

Outside, a jet roared overhead—loud, visible, celebrated.

Inside, the rules had just shifted again without anyone asking whether that was allowed.

The line hadn't moved because someone crossed it.

It moved because the system realized the line no longer protected what it was supposed to.

And that meant one thing:

The next move wouldn't be about speed.
Or noise.
Or permission.

It would be about **who told the story first**.

Kade looked at the quiet machines in the hangar—at the Lear, the 210, the tools that had asked better questions than anyone expected.

"Good," he said softly. "Now we're where timing matters."

Zara nodded.

"And where mistakes get expensive," she said.

Kade smiled faintly.

"That's why we won't make one," he replied.

The line had moved.

And Kade was already standing on the safe side of it—because he'd never treated it as real in the first place.

Chapter 29

DISCLOSURE

They didn't call it a release.

That word implied permission.

They called it a **technical note**.

Four pages. No branding. No press conference. No dramatic conclusions. Just methodology, assumptions, and repeatable results—written in the plain, unromantic language that engineers trusted and politicians hated.

Zara uploaded it at 02:14 local.

Three repositories.
Two mirrors.
One delayed public index.

No headlines.

Yet.

Kade stood behind her, hands in his pockets, watching the progress bar crawl forward like a heartbeat.

"This is the point of no return," Zara said quietly.

Kade nodded. "We passed that a while ago. This is just where everyone else notices."

The document didn't say *underground structures*.

It didn't say *cover-up*.

It didn't even say *supersonic*.

Instead, it said things like:

Observed pressure coherence within high-subsonic transitional regimes demonstrates repeatable subsurface response sensitivity beyond existing GPR resolution limits.

And:

Results suggest non-invasive mapping potential under specific velocity and atmospheric coupling conditions.

No accusations.
No politics.
No finger-pointing.

Just physics.

Zara hit **Publish**.

Nothing happened.

For six minutes, the world stayed exactly the same.

Then the first pull appeared.

A university in Norway.
An energy lab in Alberta.
A civil engineering firm in Japan.

Zara watched the requests populate quietly.

"They're reading," she said.

Kade smiled faintly. "Good ones always do."

By morning, the second wave arrived.

Defense contractors—masked as research entities.
Infrastructure consortiums.
Seismic modeling firms that hadn't updated their public sites in years.

No comments.
No questions.

Just downloads.

Zara leaned back in her chair.

"They understand it," she said.

"Yes," Kade replied. "And that terrifies the wrong people."

The first public mention appeared twelve hours later.

Not a headline.

A footnote.

A senior geophysicist cited the paper during a virtual conference, almost offhandedly, as a *curious but promising extension of transonic sensing theory*.

No applause.

No pushback.

Which meant the room had gone very still.

By the next day, the system reacted.

Not with denials.

With *reframing*.

A government white paper appeared referencing "emerging civilian sensing concepts," carefully crediting "multiple independent research threads."

Zara laughed once when she saw it.

"They're trying to absorb it," she said.

Kade nodded. "That's phase two."

The oil sector moved faster.

An internal memo leaked—accidentally, of course—outlining *cost-saving potential in non-invasive reservoir characterization*.

Zara pulled it up side by side with their original map.

"They see the money," she said.

"And missed the warning," Kade replied.

The warning wasn't in the data.

It was in the *implication*.

You couldn't selectively map the ground.

You mapped *everything*.

Cities.
Tunnels.
Infrastructure no one admitted existed anymore.

Zara closed her laptop slowly.

"They can't put this back," she said.

"No," Kade agreed. "And they won't try."

Because suppression required secrecy.

And secrecy required silence.

This had neither.

The hangar was quiet that evening, the kind of quiet that followed a storm you hadn't heard but could feel in the pressure of the air. Maggie slept under the wing. The Lear sat unchanged. The 210 waited like it always had.

Nothing looked different.

Everything was.

"They're going to say this was inevitable," Zara said.

Kade smiled faintly.

"They always do," he replied. "After they lose control."

She looked at him.

"Are you worried?" she asked.

Kade considered the question.

"No," he said finally. "I'm relieved."

"Because?" she pressed.

"Because now," he said, "it belongs to reality. Not permission."

Outside, a jet climbed into the sky—loud, celebrated, irrelevant.

Inside, the quiet truth spread without asking anyone if that was allowed.

Disclosure hadn't come with a bang.

It came with documentation.

And that was worse for anyone who thought speed was the danger.

Because once something could be measured, repeated, and taught—

It stopped being deniable.

Chapter 30

AFTER THE BOOM

There was no boom.

That was what surprised people the most.

No alarms. No emergency sessions broadcast live. No sudden grounding of fleets or midnight speeches. The world didn't stop. Markets opened. Flights departed. Coffee was poured. Meetings started five minutes late like they always did.

The change moved *through* the system, not *at* it.

Kade noticed it in the way people stopped arguing.

The week after the technical note circulated, the loudest voices went quiet. The pundits pivoted. The confident denials softened into "interesting questions" and "areas for further study."

No one said *wrong* anymore.

They said *early*.

Zara tracked the shift from the hangar, a wall of screens showing nothing dramatic and everything important.

"They've accepted the premise," she said.

Kade nodded. "That's when things get real."

Acceptance didn't look like agreement. It looked like funding lines quietly redirected. Job postings rewritten with new language. Research grants reframed to chase answers that hadn't existed on paper a month earlier.

Civil engineers started asking different questions.

Urban planners, too.

Zara pulled up a municipal request for proposals from a mid-sized European city.

"Non-invasive subsurface characterization for infrastructure resilience," she read. "No drilling."

Kade smiled faintly.

"Boring," he said.

"Exactly," Zara replied.

Boring was victory.

Because boring meant normalized.

The oil sector tried to move faster—and paid for it.

A major firm announced a pilot program, touting "novel transonic data correlations" without citing the source. Their stock jumped briefly. Then analysts started asking questions they couldn't answer.

The program was shelved within days.

"They don't understand the coupling," Zara said.

"No," Kade agreed. "They understand leverage. That's not the same thing."

Governments moved differently.

Not by banning anything. Not by announcing new rules. Instead, they layered process on top of process—committees, reviews, interagency task forces with names that sounded reassuring and meant delay.

But even delay had a cost now.

Because universities weren't waiting.

Neither were independent labs.

The physics worked whether anyone liked it or not.

Kade flew the 210 less that month. Not because he was hiding—because there was no need. The sky had returned to being just the sky. Mach numbers were discussed in journals again, not memos.

The Lear stayed in the hangar, unchanged, patient.

A tool that had already done its job.

One afternoon, Zara closed her laptop and leaned back, eyes tired but satisfied.

"They're teaching it," she said.

Kade looked up. "Teaching what?"

"The method," she replied. "Stripped down. Sanitized. No history."

Kade nodded slowly.

"That's fine," he said. "History's heavy."

She studied him for a moment.

"They'll never credit you," she said.

Kade smiled.

"They already did," he replied.

"How?"

"They stopped trying to stop it."

That night, Kade sat on the tailgate of Frank's old truck, the hangar lights low, Maggie curled at his feet. The air was still. Ordinary. Perfect.

He thought about Yeager—not the hero version, not the myth—but the pilot who'd felt something strange and written it down anyway. About Frank, who'd trusted the land to tell the truth if you listened long enough.

The world hadn't ended.

It had adjusted.

And that was always the more dangerous outcome.

Zara joined him outside, handing him a beer.

"To boring," she said.

Kade clinked it lightly.

"To boring," he agreed.

They drank in silence, listening to the distant sound of a jet climbing hard, fast, and watched by everyone who still believed speed was the story.

Kade didn't look up.

After the boom, nothing needed to be loud.

Because the ground was answering questions now—everywhere, all the time.

And once a system learned how to listen…

It never forgot.

Chapter 31

WHAT STAYS BURIED

The last attempt didn't come with threats.

That surprised Kade more than anything else.

No black SUVs. No subpoenas. No men in suits asking polite questions with sharp edges underneath. Instead, it arrived as a request buried so deep in bureaucratic language it barely registered as intent.

Zara found it first, of course.

She didn't say anything right away. Just slid her chair back, stood, and walked to the hangar door, staring out at the runway like she needed to ground herself before speaking.

"They want a boundary," she said finally.

Kade looked up from the workbench. "Define want."

"They're asking for exclusion zones," she said. "Not airspace. *Knowledge*."

That got his attention.

She turned the screen toward him. The document was real—real enough to be dangerous. A draft framework, never meant to be seen outside a narrow circle. It proposed limitations on application, not discovery. Areas where the new methods would be considered "destabilizing" if applied.

Urban cores.
Legacy infrastructure.
Certain geographic regions that didn't appear in any public risk analysis.

"They're not trying to stop it," Kade said quietly.

"No," Zara replied. "They're trying to *shape* what stays invisible."

Kade studied the list.

Some of the regions made sense—densely layered cities where revelation would cause panic, lawsuits, chaos. Others made no sense at all unless you knew what *wasn't* supposed to be known.

Old sites.
Old tunnels.
Old decisions.

"They're afraid of context," Kade said.

Zara nodded. "They can survive exposure. They can't survive understanding."

Kade leaned back, eyes on the ceiling.

This was the part no one talked about in discovery stories. Not the breakthrough. Not the fight. The *aftermath*, where you learned what the world could absorb—and what it couldn't.

"You know," Zara said carefully, "this is where people usually make a deal."

Kade smiled faintly. "I know."

"They'll call it responsible stewardship," she continued. "Ethics. Stability."

"And mean control," Kade finished.

She met his gaze.

"Are they wrong?" she asked.

The question hung between them—not as a challenge, but as something real.

Kade didn't answer right away.

He thought about the map. About what it showed and what it implied. About cities built on layers of assumption. About secrets that had become load-bearing.

"There are things," he said finally, "that don't get safer just because they're true."

Zara nodded slowly.

"And there are truths," she said, "that break more than they fix."

Silence settled.

Outside, a jet passed overhead, loud enough to shake the hangar doors for a second before fading into distance.

Kade stood and walked to the whiteboard, wiping it clean except for one word he wrote deliberately.

RESPONSIBILITY

"This isn't about hiding," he said. "It's about *sequence*."

Zara studied the word.

"So what stays buried?" she asked.

Kade turned back to her.

"Anything that turns knowledge into a weapon before people understand it," he said. "Anything that collapses trust faster than it builds truth."

She exhaled.

"That's a heavy line to draw."

"Yes," Kade said. "Which is why it can't belong to them."

Zara looked at the document again.

"What do we do?" she asked.

Kade considered it.

Then he smiled—not amused, not defiant. Certain.

"We publish the boundary," he said. "And the reasoning."

Zara blinked. "You want to *explain* restraint?"

"Yes," Kade replied. "Because the moment restraint is visible, it stops being control."

She thought about that, then nodded slowly.

"They won't like that," she said.

"They don't have to," Kade replied. "They just won't own it."

They drafted the response together—measured, calm, unassailable. Acknowledging limits. Emphasizing ethics. Framing restraint as an evolving conversation, not a closed door.

No exclusions without explanation.
No silence without accountability.

By the time they sent it, the sun had dipped low, the hangar bathed in amber light.

Zara closed her laptop.

"That's it," she said. "They'll back off."

Kade nodded. "And they'll watch."

"Always."

He looked around the hangar—the Lear, the 210, the quiet tools, the machines that had asked questions without caring who approved them.

"Some things," he said, "don't need to be dug up to matter."

Zara smiled faintly.

"And some things," she added, "stay buried because we choose not to be careless."

Kade met her gaze.

"That's the difference between power and responsibility," he said.

Outside, the ground remained quiet.

Not because it was hiding.

But because, for now, it didn't need to speak.

Epilogue

JUST BELOW MACH

Kade flew alone.

No Zara. No mission. No data collection humming quietly in the background. Just him, the airplane, and the sky the way it had always been before anyone started asking it questions.

The 210 climbed steadily, familiar as breath. The engine settled into a rhythm Kade had trusted for most of his life. Below him, the land stretched out—fields, ridges, water catching light in ways no satellite ever quite captured.

He leveled off and trimmed for cruise.

Mach didn't matter today.

He wasn't listening for patterns. He wasn't watching numbers. He let the airplane do what it was built to do and let his mind wander where it needed to go.

He thought about Frank, about Yeager, about all the men who'd flown into the unknown not because they wanted attention, but because something in them refused to ignore a question once it appeared.

The rule was still there.

Don't break Mach.

Not because it couldn't be done.

But because some thresholds changed the conversation in ways you couldn't take back.

Kade smiled to himself.

Just below Mach was where the truth whispered instead of shouted. Where you could hear it without waking everyone else up.

The world hadn't ended.

It hadn't been saved, either.

It had adjusted—incrementally, quietly, the way all real change did.

Kade glanced at the horizon, then down at the land once more.

It looked the same.

It wasn't.

And that was okay.

He pushed the throttle forward just enough to feel the airplane respond—not racing, not daring. Alive.

Just below the line.

Right where he belonged.

End of Book EIGHT

About the Author:

Kevin Seney is a pilot, investigator, and lifelong storyteller with a background in business intelligence and a passion for exploring what lies beneath the surface—of both people and places. A former CEO and licensed private investigator, he now writes full time from his home base in the American West, where the skies are wide, and the stories never stay grounded for long.

When he's not restoring vintage trucks or chasing down legacy trails, he's crafting cinematic, emotionally charged adventures for readers who believe love is worth fighting for—and truth is worth chasing.

He lives in Park City, Utah, with his wife Carrie, their six daughters, and two German Shorthair Pointers—Maggie and Aspen—writing fiction that blends romance, mystery, legacy, and the kind of truth that follows you long after the last page.

Kade Vance
The Runway Rogue

One man's road to redemption winds through love, loss… and the echoes of a forgotten legacy.

After a high-stakes career and a fractured past, pilot and investigator Kade Vance set off with nothing but his dog Maggie, a hangar full of ghosts, and a mission to rebuild his life—mile by mile. From the California coast to the American South, and deep into the heart of Central America, his search for clarity became something more: a spiral of love, memory, and purpose that could change everything.

But the truth didn't just live in his past. It was waiting to be uncovered—in an old family ledger, a sealed map hidden in his grandfather's Cessna… and a final message that would send him into the sky once more.

Meet Me in Savannah began the journey.
The Seven Echoes of the Lost World changed the mission. Now, the compass is still ticking—and Kade's story is just beginning.

For fans of Nicholas Sparks, Rebecca Yarros, and Taylor Sheridan, this romantic adventure blends emotional depth, slow-burn suspense, and cinematic grit.

Sometimes the road home… is the one you never planned to take.

Made in the USA
Coppell, TX
13 January 2026

68225067R10166